"It's very [obscured by barcode] go to all this tr[obscured] on't suppose y[obscured]den somewhere, [obscured]

If Ryan was frustrated by her refusal, he didn't show it. Despite the heat, he remained cool and collected. "Fine. I had hoped that you felt something, like I did. And I'd hoped it could turn into more if we gave it a chance. But I won't push you on that. You have every right to your feelings."

She sighed, relief flooding through her body. She didn't need this to be any more awkward than it already was. Feelings would just make things messier. "Good. Then we agree we need to approach this from a purely logistic standpoint."

"I'm glad you said that. Because I have a plan B for you."

"And what is that?"

Pleased with the more reasonable turn to the conversation, Jessica took a deep drink from her now-cooled coffee.

"A marriage of convenience."

Dear Reader,

Welcome back to Paradise! For such a sleepy little island, it sure has its share of big personalities, and Deputy Jessica Santiago is no exception!

You might remember her brother, Deputy Alex Santiago, from *A Valentine for a Veterinarian*—and if so, you'll know that Jessica's stubborn streak of independence is a family trait. She's not one to let anyone or anything stand in her way. But when her first day on the job involves the return of a former lover, a physical assault by a drunken criminal *and* a surprise diagnosis she never expected, she has to accept that everyone needs a little help, sometimes.

As you may know by now, surprise pregnancies are a favorite story line for me—and really, *every* pregnancy has its own surprises. Impending motherhood forces you to accept the unexpected, and there is *plenty* of that in this book. I even threw in a surprise from Mother Nature, one that creates the setup for my favorite scene ever—a moment that captures the power and strength innate in every woman.

I hope as you read this you are reminded of the joy that comes from all the twists and turns that life throws at us, and of the strength we find when we embrace the adventure of it all.

Happy reading!

Katie Meyer

PS: I love to connect with my readers! Follow me on Facebook and Twitter, send me an email, or check out my website!

www.KatieMeyerBooks.com

www.Facebook.com/KatieMeyerBooks

www.Twitter.com/ktgrok

katiemeyerbooks@gmail.com

The Marriage Moment

KATIE MEYER

HARLEQUIN
SPECIAL
EDITION

HARLEQUIN®
SPECIAL
EDITION™

Recycling programs
for this product may
not exist in your area.

ISBN-13: 978-1-335-40463-3

The Marriage Moment

Copyright © 2020 by Katie Meyer

This edition published by arrangement with Harlequin Books S.A.

For questions and comments about the quality of this book,
please contact us at CustomerService@Harlequin.com.

Harlequin Enterprises ULC
22 Adelaide St. West, 40th Floor
Toronto, Ontario M5H 4E3, Canada
www.Harlequin.com

Printed in U.S.A.

Katie Meyer is a Florida native with a firm belief in happy endings. A former veterinary technician and dog trainer, she now spends her days homeschooling her children, writing and snuggling with her pets. Her guilty pleasures include good chocolate, *Downton Abbey* and cheap champagne. Preferably all at once. She looks to her parents' whirlwind romance and her own happy marriage for her romantic inspiration.

Books by Katie Meyer

Harlequin Special Edition

Paradise Animal Clinic

The Marriage Moment
Do You Take This Daddy?
A Valentine for the Veterinarian
The Puppy Proposal

Proposals in Paradise

The Groom's Little Girls
A Wedding Worth Waiting For

This book is dedicated to all the people who had patience with me and faith in my abilities when I wasn't sure how or when I'd ever manage to write a whole book again—especially my husband, Ean; my agent, Jill; and my editor, Carly.

Chapter One

Nothing in Deputy Jessica Santiago's training had prepared her for this moment.

Not her bachelor's degree in Criminal Justice, not her time in the police academy and certainly not the packet of training materials she'd memorized before starting her first shift as a deputy in the Palmetto County sheriff's department. Sweat trickled between her breasts under the perfectly pressed navy uniform she had so proudly put on a few hours ago, mocking her commitment to bravery in the face of danger.

But Ryan O'Sullivan wasn't the kind of threat she'd expected to face as the only female law enforcement officer to come from Paradise Isle, Florida, in nearly a decade.

What was he doing here? He wore the same uniform she did, and for a moment her face heated as she remembered exactly what he looked like without any clothes at all. But he wasn't supposed to be in Paradise. The last they'd spoken, a hurried and awkward conversation as she'd dressed herself in the early morning light, he'd told her that he'd hired on at the police department in his home town. He should have been hundreds of miles away in Miami Beach, not across the room, looking every bit as sexy as she remembered. She never would have slept with him if she'd thought there was a chance she would see him again.

Not that she had been a virgin—she'd crossed that bridge back in college with a longtime boyfriend, though that relationship had turned into a long-distance breakup when he graduated from the University of Florida a year before her and moved to Oregon. But one-night stands weren't usually her style either. She'd been raised in a religious household, and although she didn't always go along with everything the church taught, in many ways she was still the good Catholic girl her mother had raised her to be. But even an angel would have been temped by Ryan O'Sullivan.

Tall with broad shoulders that spoke of his

college swimming success, he towered over everyone else in the room. At only five foot three herself, Ryan was a full foot taller than her, but that wasn't why she'd mentally marked him off as out of reach. It was much more than that—he was the uncrowned king of the academy recruits, the kind of man who inspired admiration from other men and something a bit more visceral among the women.

Looking at him now out of the corner of her eye, it was easy to see why he'd always had a flock of females around him everywhere he went. Dark hair, classically sculpted features any male model would envy, and soulful brown eyes that were more sinful than her favorite triple-chocolate espresso cake. So yes, she'd crushed on him, as had every other woman in their class. But she'd gone to the academy to learn, not to flirt. So every time he'd asked her out she'd ignored him and focused on the job at hand. Until graduation night, when a bit too much tequila had intensified the lust she usually kept under control, overriding her better judgment.

And now she was regretting it. Because alcohol or not, had she known she'd be working in the same department with him two months later, she would have kept her clothes on and her legs crossed, no matter how intense the chemistry had been between them.

No, not chemistry. That implied a real connection, something beyond the sheer relief of finishing up such an intense training schedule—and topping off that liberating sense of freedom with a hefty dose of alcohol-lubricated lust. It was pure hedonism; nothing personal. In fact, she was probably stressing out over nothing. As many women as he'd been rumored to have been with, and as much booze as they'd shared, there was a good chance that night hadn't even registered on his radar. He likely hadn't given their encounter, or her, a second thought since then.

Clutching to that hope, she kept her eyes forward and headed for the door the minute the department meeting was over. She was to report to the staffing sergeant, where she'd be paired up with a partner and given her patrol orders for the evening. Thankfully, her brother had recently switched to day shifts; the last thing she needed was a protective older brother hovering over her on her first shift. As long as he wasn't there, she didn't care who she got partnered with.

Or maybe she did. Blocking her way into the main precinct was Ryan, a boyish grin on his face. Dread slithered through her gut. Surely they wouldn't pair up two rookies, would they?

"Jessica, I was just coming to look for you."

And I was trying to avoid you, she nearly muttered. Instead, she managed a nervous smile, and tried her hardest to forget that he'd ever seen her naked. "Well, you found me." Smooth. "I didn't expect to see you here." Or ever again.

"Jason ended up getting the post in Miami. It was kind of a last minute thing." He shrugged, his muscular shoulders stretching the limits of his department-issued uniform. "This was the only other opening left, and I remembered you talking about what a nice town Paradise was, so I figured I'd give small-town life a try."

"Oh." Of course she'd known he hadn't purposely come here to be with her, but hearing that it was his last choice didn't feel great either. "Well, I hope you like it. It's very different from Miami." She'd grown up there too, but the Little Havana neighborhood she'd called home was nothing like the wealthy suburb he came from. She'd been in college, living in the dorms, when her mom and brother picked up and moved to Paradise. Over long weekends and holiday breaks she'd gotten to know the small island, and although she still sometimes missed the excitement of Miami, Paradise was her home now.

"So I've noticed. But I figure you can show

me around, help me find the best local hangouts and such."

She blinked in surprise, but found her voice quickly. "I don't think that's a great idea." At all.

"Hey, I just meant when we're on patrol. Since we're going to be partners and all."

What? Her pulse pounded in her ears. "We can't be partners. All new recruits are supposed to be assigned to more senior deputies."

"True, but almost half the night shift is out with the flu. There just aren't enough senior deputies to go around for all us newbies. So the sergeant in there said we can either ride desks for the next few days, or partner up for the night. What do you say?"

Ryan held his breath while Jessica considered his offer. She'd left town before he'd had a chance to see her again, and he had no idea what she thought of their night together. As far as he was concerned, it had been incredible. But he'd never gotten to say so, and now she was looking at him as if she'd rather be anyplace but by his side. A few weeks ago, they'd been as close as two people could get, and now she wasn't sure she could stand one shift on patrol with him?

"What about…um, the other night?" She glanced nervously down the hall, obviously not wanting to be overheard. "Isn't there a rule about not pairing up people who have any kind of romantic connection? Not that we do, of course." Her face flushed a deeper red than he would have thought possible. "I mean, I know it was just one night. But I don't want to start off by breaking the rules."

No, she wouldn't want that. She was the kind to play things by the book—he'd learned that about her at the academy. "I told the sergeant that we'd briefly had a thing, but that it was in the past. He said he was too short-staffed to worry about old feelings, and that unless we wanted to just go home we should be grown-ups about it and get to work." He waited, breath held, to see her reaction to the pronouncement. Would she agree that things *were* entirely in the past? He wasn't entirely certain of that, himself. Certainly his instinctive reaction to her was alive and well in the present.

Jessica's sigh of relief was audible. "Okay. Hopefully he'll keep that information to himself. The last thing I need is rumors getting around."

So that was how it was going to be. Not real flattering, but if she wanted to pretend nothing had happened, he certainly wouldn't push her on the matter. At least, not at first. "Fine by me."

Relief, and something else he couldn't quite place flashed in her eyes before her features schooled themselves into the professional detachment he was used to from her. A lot of the guys had said she was cold, or worse, because of the way she carried herself. More likely, they were just annoyed she showed more interest in her coursework than she did in them. And her scores showed it—she'd been at the top of their class. As far as he was concerned, her dedication was something to be admired, not resented, even if it meant she'd spent a long time refusing his advances. Still, he'd found himself watching her more often than he liked to admit. With perfectly smooth, copper-colored skin, almond shaped brown eyes, and raven black curls that fell halfway down her back, she made grit and determination look sexy.

Even now, with her hair pulled back at the nape of her neck and wearing an androgynous uniform that tried (and failed) to hide her lush curves, he couldn't help but want her. He knew the softness of her skin, the taste of her lips, and now he was going to have to pretend they barely knew each other? He'd heard that the first few weeks on the job were hell, but this wasn't the version of torture he'd expected.

Still, he was man enough to know when his advances weren't wanted. Strictly business was what she wanted, so that was how it would have to be until and unless he could convince her otherwise.

"Here's our patrol assignment." He handed her the paper with their patrol area and held up a set of keys. "Mind if I drive?"

She cocked an eyebrow. "Don't you think I should be the one to drive, since you asked me to show you around?"

She had him there. Reluctantly, he handed the keys over. "Next time, I drive."

"You like to be in control," she observed, heading down the hall toward the exit.

"Don't you?"

She hesitated, then nodded. "Fair point. But I'm still driving."

He grinned. He could let her win for now. But if she thought she could walk all over him, she needed to think again.

In the car, she buckled herself in and then examined the paper with their area assignment again. "Looks like we'll be covering Paradise and the stretch of backroads between here and the highway." She smiled, a rare glimpse of the woman he'd briefly held in his arms. "Looks like you'll get that tour after all."

"Let's get to it then." He was glad they'd gotten that assignment for their first night. The other patrols would be working their way inland, covering the ranching towns and wilderness areas that made up the rest of eastern Palmetto County. He was a city boy, and although he would no doubt be spending plenty of time out in the boonies, he was happier in a town, even a small one like Paradise. Besides, it would give them something to talk about. He had a feeling he'd otherwise be in for a long, silent night. Maybe if he got her to open up about the island she so clearly loved, it would break whatever tension was between them and give them a chance to start over.

The sun was just sinking below the horizon as they started off, tinting the clouds with pink and gold. On Lighthouse Avenue, Paradise's version of Main Street, people were milling about, heading into restaurants for a casual meal out or hurrying home after a long day at work. Streetlights flickered, attracting swarms of moths and probably some mosquitos. Summer was still a month off, but you'd never know it from the temperature, or the beach-casual clothes everyone seemed to be wearing.

Compared to Miami, where fashion was king, it was jarring to see people in cut-offs and tank tops going about their business. "People don't dress up much here, do they?"

"Not unless you count name brand sunglasses or rhinestone flip-flops." Jessica grinned. "When most people have known each other since they were in diapers, dressing to impress doesn't make much sense, I guess."

He smiled at the idea. "Good point. I may need to downgrade my wardrobe a bit, or I'm going to look out of place." Not that he wore three-piece suits or anything, but his designer dress pants and shirts were probably going to be overkill.

"Casual clothes are a lot easier on a cop's salary," she pointed out practically.

"That's the truth." A small-town deputy didn't make much money and his parents had stopped subsidizing him when he graduated from college. "I used up most of my savings to cover the tuition for the academy. My parents would have helped out for law school, but as my stepfather said, they weren't shelling out a dime just for me to be a beat cop." He shrugged. "I expected as much from him, but thought my mom might have sided with me, considering my dad wore a badge for almost twenty years."

"So your stepfather disapproved—but didn't your Dad stick up for you?"

Ryan swallowed hard against the emotion that was still strong, even after all these years. "He *was* a cop. Past tense. He had a heart attack the year before I started high school. A freak congenital thing they said, although I don't imagine his affinity for fried food helped much either. When Mom remarried, she moved up the criminal justice ladder to a lawyer."

"Hence the push for you to attend law school?"

"Exactly. What about you, is your family supportive?"

Jessica's laugh in response was without mirth. "That's not exactly the word I would choose."

Ryan kept silent, obviously waiting for her to elaborate.

She might as well fill him in. It wasn't like there were any secrets in a small town like Paradise, less so in the law enforcement community. "My dad wasn't around much when I was growing up. He loved us, but he didn't know how to settle down. He was always chasing the next adventure, betting that the next risk was the one that would pay off. But it never did. He lived hard, and he died young, leaving mom to pick up the slack, to shoulder all the responsibility that came with being a real parent." She shrugged. "She pretty much raised my brother and me on her own, and worries like you'd expect her to. My brother, on the other hand…" She trailed off, trying to find the words. "He's on a mission to help me find something—anything—else to do with my life."

Confusion furrowed his brow "But isn't your brother a deputy himself?"

She resisted the urge to roll her eyes. "Yup. Trust me, we've had the 'pot, meet kettle' conversation more than a few times."

"Sounds like there's a story there."

She put the blinker on, then turned off the main drag and onto the road that led to the public park. "Not really. He's just a typical, overprotective big brother. He thinks he needs to take care of me—to save me from myself."

"Ah, I see. And Big Brother thinks his chosen career is too dangerous for his baby sister?"

She couldn't hide her grimace as she thought back to all the arguments they'd had on the subject. She prided herself on her self-control, but her big brother had a way of getting a rise out of her. "That's exactly what he thinks." If Alex had his way, she'd be working in an office somewhere, where the biggest risk was a paper cut. "But he's backed off recently, mostly because my mom made him. He might be tough, but she's tougher."

"So determined women run in your family. Sounds like he's outnumbered."

"You could say that." She drove a slow lap around the park, looking for anything or anyone out of place. A few older teens were shooting baskets, and a young couple had their heads together on a bench, but other than that the place was pretty much deserted. Heading away from downtown she turned onto the beach road that bordered the eastern edge of the island.

Here along the dunes the night was pitch black, her headlights the only illumination. It was like being on the edge of the world, which in some ways, it was. Beyond that cloak of darkness the sea stretched all the way to Africa. "I hadn't realized how much I missed the ocean while at school."

"Yeah, Gainesville is a great town, but if you grow up by the sea I don't think you ever can be happy living away from it."

"I think you're right." She reluctantly steered west and away from the water, heading for the bridge to the mainland. A maze of backroads ran up and down the coast, mostly leading to fishing shacks, bait shops and the occasional home. A quiet area, but also secluded enough to hide the occasional poaching shack or teenage keg party. "What made you go to UF, rather than somewhere down south?"

"Same as you, I bet. Their criminal justice program is one of the best in the nation. I didn't want to be one of those cops who are just in it for the sirens and the gun, you know? I wanted to really learn the law, to be the best law enforcement officer I could be." He shrugged, the movement illuminated by the glow of the instrument panel. "I know that sounds corny."

"No, it doesn't." She understood what he meant. It was true, you could technically become a cop with no more than a GED and six months of academy training, but the field was moving past that. "You see it as a profession, a career, not just a job." And given what he'd said about his family, maybe a way to honor his father as well?

"I do. Maybe it's not as impressive to many as a law degree, but I want the badge to mean something."

"Hey, those lawyers wouldn't have a job if we didn't enforce the law. There are differences, but at the end of the day you need both, like, two sides of the same coin. I'm surprised your stepfather can't see that."

"It's okay. Honestly, I think he's still stuck in a different time, when people who became cops didn't have an education beyond high school. For him, if you can handle academics well enough to go to college, that meant you should do something better." He smiled wryly. "Or at least something that pays better."

She winced. "I still say law enforcement is as good a job as any, but the salary part is hard to argue with. Especially considering how expensive college tuition has gotten."

"That's why I had to get a scholarship. I couldn't justify taking on debt when it would take so long to pay it off on a cop's salary. And even if he'd been willing to help out, I wasn't going to take his money when I knew he didn't approve of my career choice."

"Same here—about the scholarship I mean." She hadn't considered that he might have been on a scholarship too. From the start she'd pegged him as a rich kid riding on his parents' dime. He'd certainly dressed the part, with designer labels from head to toe. But it seemed she'd read him wrong. He might have money, but he came from working-class stock same as her. And he was paying his own way, despite his family's current wealth. If she was going to be worthy of that shiny new badge on her chest she'd need to stop making assumptions based on appearances.

The crackle of a radio signal ended her thought process, the dispatcher's words sending a shot of adrenaline into her system.

Drunk and disorderly at Pete's Crab Shack. Suspect possibly armed.

"Didn't we just pass that place?" Ryan asked, his voice tight with anticipation.

"Yes." She swung the car around, her stomach roiling at the sudden motion. She'd been dealing with a nervous stomach all week, anticipating her first day on the job, and the shock of seeing Ryan had made it worse. She'd grab some antacids later.

First she had a job to do, and she wasn't going to let a few butterflies in her stomach interfere with her job.

Chapter Two

As Jessica deftly turned the cruiser around and headed back toward the beach, Ryan tried to keep his mind on the scene they were approaching and not on the woman sitting beside him. He'd worked hard for this moment, but it wasn't the lights and siren making his heart pound and his palms sweat. No, that had started way before the call came in, courtesy of a certain feisty brunette. One with the smoothest skin he'd ever seen. Or touched, for that matter.

And touching her had been a huge mistake. Not because he hadn't enjoyed it, but because a one-night stand wasn't how you told a girl you were genuinely interested in her. And he was definitely interested. At first she'd been a challenge, and he loved a good challenge. She'd avoided his every advance, seemingly oblivious to the passes he or their other classmates made. And plenty of them had been interested in the curvy Latina. But she'd shut everyone out, resulting in mean-spirited rumors that she must be frigid or a man-hater. Though the women had been a bit kinder in their assessments, they'd also considered her standoffish since she was rarely interested in going out to parties or clubs. But he'd recognized that she wasn't trying to be cold or unfriendly. She was just busy working her butt off—a trait he respected even if he found her lack of interest in him a source of frustration.

And now, after only a short time with her, he was kicking himself for blowing his chances by letting things go too far, too fast. If they'd spent that last night at the academy talking and getting to know each other rather than falling into bed, maybe they'd be in a different place right now. Instead, he was all too aware that even referring to what had happened between them could be taken as sexual harassment. And she'd made it clear she wasn't comfortable with the topic. Once again, the barriers that she'd put around herself were in place, and he was on the outside looking in.

Karma was funny that way. Normally he was the one putting up a hard wall, making it clear to a woman that once the night was over so were they. Never with malice, and always after explaining the situation up front. He didn't mislead women— they knew before things got intimate that he wasn't ready for happily-ever-after. But sometimes things got a bit complicated and he'd have to give the speech Jessica had given him just a bit ago, about keeping what happened between them in the past. Now, he was the one wanting more and getting the door slammed politely but firmly in his face.

Not the best feeling in the world. Especially since he was still drawn to her. Physically and on every other level.

But there was nothing to be done about it— not now anyway. He needed to stay focused on their first call. Scanning the info on the built-in computer screen he read the few details available. Seemed a patron who'd had a few too many long-necks got angry about being cut off and started yelling threats, prompting one of the bartenders to call 911.

Hopefully it was just a matter of angry words, but the caller had been right to take it seriously. Nothing was as unpredictable as a person under the influence of drugs or alcohol. A little bit of liquid courage could lower anyone's inhibitions. Hell, his night with Jessica was proof of that.

Darting a glance at her, he envied her composure. If it wasn't for the speed she coaxed from the car you would have thought she was out for a Sunday drive, not headed straight into possible mayhem. Meanwhile adrenaline churned through his own body, increasing with each mile they covered.

Any minute now their training and skills would be put to their first true test. He'd need to keep himself, the public and his partner safe against an as-yet-unknown foe. He could only hope he was up to the challenge. Despite their hard work, they were both rookies heading into a dangerous situation.

The odds were in their favor, but lady luck didn't always play fair. He said a silent prayer asking that she be on their side tonight.

Jessica pulled into the parking lot of the restaurant, parking directly in front of the weathered wooden steps that went up to the dining area. A local institution, Pete's Crab Shack boasted the freshest seafood, coldest beer and biggest burgers in town, and was a popular nightspot with both residents and tourists alike. Despite the ramshackle look of the building, the place was well run and family friendly. At least, it normally was. Tonight was apparently an exception.

She radioed in that they were on scene, determined to do everything by the book. As the only woman on the force she needed to prove herself—not just as a rookie but as the supposedly weaker sex. The only way to do that was to be even tougher, more professional and more in control than the guys she worked with. Any sign of weakness would and could be used against her—and any other woman in uniform.

That was why the very last thing she needed was even a rumor of a workplace romance. That would be exactly the kind of argument used to lobby against women and men working together. Proof that women would let their hormones take priority over duty—further evidence that women didn't have the strength or smarts to handle the job.

Through all the "jokes," and insults and actual sexual harassment she'd experienced on her journey to becoming a cop, she'd learned that to be taken seriously meant being more controlled and professional than the men in her class. It wasn't easy, but she'd done it, bottling up every last bit of emotion. With her family and friends she could be her normal, opinionated self. But at work, it was all business. There was no other option when both her career and public safety were on the line.

Which was why she refused to acknowledge the tingle of anticipation that coursed through her body as she exited the vehicle and started for the stairs. At least the excitement of her first real call had chased away the butterflies that had been dive-bombing in her belly all day.

Ryan matched her step for step as she scanned their surroundings. Halfway up a waitress met them, her eyes wide with fear. "Oh thank God you're here. That guy's out of control!"

"Anna," Jessica said, reading the woman's name tag, "I need you to stay calm and tell us what's going on."

The waitress nodded, swallowing hard. "It's Bill. He's one of the regulars. Usually he's no trouble but lately he's been hitting the booze harder than usual. I heard someone say tonight that his wife left him. When Denny—that's the bartender—cut him off, he started yelling that everyone was out to get him and he wasn't going to take it anymore. He knocked down the manager when she tried to get him to leave, and now he's out on the patio screaming nonsense and won't let anyone get near him."

"Is he armed?" Ryan asked, his eyes darting to the top of the stairs.

"No, at least I don't think so. But he's a big guy—not fat, but big. You know, like a football

player. I think he works construction or something." She glanced back over her shoulder, as if
checking to be sure he hadn't followed her.

"Can you tell me where he is on the patio, exactly?" Jessica asked, as she tried to call up a men-
tal image of the restaurant floor plan.

"To the left of the stairs, between here and the
bar."

Damn. If there had been a way to get the other
patrons out and away from the scene, that would
have been best. But his position meant any diners
would have to walk right past him to get to the
stairs, which were the only real exit. In an emergency they could use the fire escape off the back,
but it would take three times as long and she didn't
want to risk anyone slipping and getting hurt—
or worse, getting trampled in a stampede. Which
meant whatever was about to happen, they were
going to have an audience full of untrained by-
standers.

Ryan nodded at the waitress. "Thanks, Anna.
We'll take it from here."

Leaving the distraught waitress behind they
made their way toward the dining area. Jessica
listened, hoping to hear some kind of clue as to
what they are walking into, but the reggae music
playing over the loudspeakers drowned out every-

thing else. At the top of the stairs they paused, looking for their man.

Jessica spotted him first. "Over there, against the railing."

"I see him. Let's go slow, maybe we can talk some sense into him."

She nodded in agreement. Maybe just seeing the uniforms would shock the guy out of his rant and make him see reason. He looked to be in his late thirties or early forties, with dark scraggly hair that curled over the ratty collar of his stained T-shirt and the beginnings of a beer gut straining the limits of his cut-off shorts. But the waitress was right, there was plenty of muscle underneath that paunch. Right now he was mumbling something she couldn't quite make out, pacing beside the railing that surrounded the raised deck that served as the restaurant's seating area.

"Excuse me, Bill?" Jessica stepped forward and forced a smile, hoping a soft touch might keep things from turning ugly. "Can we talk for a minute?"

At the sound of his name he turned toward her, something glinting in his hand. Shifting to get a better view, she realized it was a bottle. A broken-off beer bottle. As weapons went, it was crude, but more than capable of doing serious damage.

"Careful," Ryan warned, "He's got a—"

"I see it." Jessica kept her eyes glued to the man in front of her. "Bill, can you put down that bottle for me? You don't want anyone to get hurt, do you?"

His eyes were bloodshot, glazed over with either anger or liquor or both, but for a second she thought he might actually listen. But then, instead of putting the weapon down, he raised it in an obvious threat. "You bitch! You're just like my wife, thinking you can boss me around. Well, I'll show you what happens to bossy women who don't know their place!" And then, in the space of a heartbeat, he lunged straight for her.

Ryan shouted out a warning, his own voice echoing in his ears as he watched the drunken jerk plow toward Jessica, the jagged edges of the bottle aimed straight for her chest. Ryan reached for his Taser. Gunshots were likely to make the situation worse rather than better, especially in a crowded location. Bullets had a way of finding the worst possible landing place. A Taser was not always effective, but at least it was safe in a crowd.

But even as he jerked the device from his belt he knew he wouldn't be able to use it in time. The other man was too fast, and too close. The best he could hope for was to immobilize him after the fact. He shouldn't have let Jessica be the one to draw the man's wrath. It should have been him, not her.

It all took maybe a second, but felt like a life-time, everything happening in torturous slow motion—the perp's angry lunge, his own shouted warning, the diners behind him scrambling for cover.

"Get back!" Jessica yelled, and then, right in front of his eyes, she defied gravity. At least, it looked that way as she somehow sidestepped and ducked, grabbing the perp's arm and flipping him over her shoulder as if he'd grown wings and a sincere desire to fly.

The landing, however, was less smooth. Ryan barely managed to avoid being squashed by the lumberjack of a man, and Jessica got tripped up in his tree trunk—like legs, going down in a heap, half her body under his.

Not wanting to give the idiot a chance to get up and do more damage, Ryan refastened the Taser to his equipment belt and grabbed his cuffs, using the man's momentary disorientation to secure his hands behind his back. The fall must have knocked the wind out of him, because other than a pained moan the man was still and quiet, his hefty weight pinning Jessica to the ground. His broken-bottle weapon was nowhere in sight, but at least Ryan could be sure it was no longer in his hands. Quickly

Ryan tapped his radio and called for an ambulance. "Possible officer down," he added, praying he was being overly cautious.

"Oomph. Get him off me." Her head and upper torso were visible, but her lower body was trapped. Grabbing both her small wrists with one of his hands, he used the other to lift the perp's body a few inches, sliding her out. She kneeled, panting, and shook her head, her carefully pinned-back hair now flying in the wind. A button had come loose on her shirt, and there was a dark stain on her abdomen.

Blood?

Oh hell, she was bleeding. The bastard had gotten her. Hitting the ground hard he yanked her shirt from her pants and started unbuttoning it from the bottom, searching for the wound. He needed to find it and stop the bleeding, ASAP. Who knew how long it would take the paramedics to get out to this stretch of beach road.

Jessica batted at his hands. "What the hell do you think you're doing?" She shoved at his chest. "Get back, or I swear, I'll knock you down too."

"I need to find out where he cut you."

"What?" She looked down at herself in confusion. "I'm fine."

"No, you're not." Hell, that wasn't the right thing to say. He needed her to stay calm. "I mean,

I'm sure you will be. But you're bleeding." He'd heard that in the moment adrenaline could mask the pain of an injury. She must be going into shock. He peeled the red stained fabric away from her flat stomach desperate now to find the source of all that blood. Naturally bronzed skin peeked out, skin he'd explored under much different circumstances less than two months ago. He found smears of blood, but no wound.

Jessica grabbed the edges of the fabric and yanked them closed. "That's not my blood, you idiot."

"What?" Confused, his fingers stopped of their own accord.

"I said, it's NOT. MY. BLOOD." She shoved against the body of her attacker next to her, grunting as she strained to roll Bill onto his back. "The jerk fell on his own damn weapon."

Ryan lent his own strength to the effort, and sure enough, the perp's shirt was dark with blood, a tear revealing the ragged edges of flesh that had been ravaged by the broken bottle he'd wielded. It was a gruesome wound, but as horrified as Ryan knew he should be, all he could feel was relief that it wasn't Jessica's insides spilling out.

"Sorry, I thought he'd gotten you," Ryan offered in apology. Turning back to her, he expected to see her buttoning her shirt and looking annoyed.

Instead, her skin was white, her eyes glassy where they focused on the blood and gore coming from her attacker.

"Jessica, are you okay?" Maybe she'd been nicked after all.

She blinked once, and then her eyes rolled back in her head as her body fell forward into his arms.

Chapter Three

It was the sirens that woke her, wailing their way into her half-conscious mind. Was that her alarm clock? But that didn't seem right.

Gradually she became aware of someone talking to her, but the words were garbled, as if the person was speaking from very far away, or under water. Whatever they were saying, she wanted them to go away. She didn't want to wake up, not yet.

"Jessica! Wake up, come on baby, I need you to wake up."

He was shaking her now, whoever he was. Annoyed, she summoned the strength to open first one eye, then the other. "Ryan?" Was she dreaming about him again? Ever since their night together she'd had the most erotic dreams about him, ones that left her hot and flushed when she woke. She blinked, and realized there was a crowd around them. That definitely wasn't part of her fantasies.

Which meant this was real.

She struggled to free herself from his arms as she fought a rush of nausea.

"Easy there, champ. The paramedics are on their way. Just hold still another minute for me."

Paramedics? What the hell was going on? She pulled away just a few inches, more carefully this time, needing to see what was going on—no easy feat given the way everything was spinning. Or was she the one spinning? "What happened?"

"You passed out. You must have hit your head when that oaf fell on you."

She thought back, remembering the call, the man with bottle. She'd taken him down. But she hadn't hit her head. Had she? She gingerly moved it.

No more dizziness, and when she ran a hand through her hair there were no tender spots. "Nothing hurts."

"Yeah, well, let's let the medics decide that."

"Seriously, you shouldn't have called them. I'm fine." Glancing down, she hastily rebuttoned her ruined shirt, hoping he didn't see the way her hands shook.

"Like I said, you passed out. That's not fine. Besides, I had to called them for him, anyway."

She darted a look over at the man lying beside her and her stomach lurched. Crap, that's why she'd fainted. She hadn't hit her head, she'd gone down at the sight of his injury. Fainting when faced with blood. That wasn't going to do her reputation any favors. Averting her gaze, she focused on the steps, where white-uniformed medics where carrying a stretcher toward them.

"Take him, I'm fine." To prove it, she shoved to her feet, nearly toppling over at the sudden movement. Ryan gripped her shoulder and glared at her before addressing the medical team. "Shc's going to the hospital too. She lost consciousness after that moron fell on top of her. She could have a concussion or something."

"I'm telling you, my head is fine. It's probably just low blood sugar. I was busy today and didn't get a chance to eat dinner before starting my shift." Truth was, first-day nerves meant she'd been too nauseated to eat the spicy bean dish her mom had made for her, but she couldn't admit that in front of Ryan. She'd already proven herself weak enough to faint, no need to add to the stigma by confessing to anxiety, as well.

"And if that's the case, I'm sure they can give you something to eat when you get to the hospital. But you're going if I have to cuff you to the ambulance." His tone was even, but firm.

"You could try, but as I think I've shown, big men don't scare me."

His mouth quirked up in a wry grin. "So I saw. And once the docs clear you, I'm going to have you teach me whatever magic you used to flip that guy."

"That wasn't magic, it was aikido. I started taking lessons when I was thirteen and a high school basketball player tried to pull me into his car for a bit of one-on-one." She grinned. "Turned out he needed to learn how to guard his balls a bit better. But I knew it might not be that easy to get away from the next guy, so I found an instructor, and learned to protect myself."

"And you did a damn good job of it."

She grimaced. "Yeah, but momentum and leverage can only do so much. I'll have a few bruises in the morning."

"They can check those out at the hospital too." He raised a hand, stalling the argument she'd been about to make. "Forget about it, Santiago. You're not going to change my mind. If nothing else, there is going to be an incident report. The higher-ups will want documentation that you are fit to return to duty."

Crap, he was right. If she tried to get out of it now, she'd just end up having to see a doctor tomorrow. Might as well get it over with. "Okay. But no ambulance." There was no way she was going to let herself be strapped in next to a guy whose insides were now on the outside. Normally she wasn't squeamish, but today seemed to be an exception.

Ryan must have realized he'd pushed her as far as he could, because he gave a reluctant nod. "Fine, if the paramedics say you can wait I'll drive you over myself, after I get the witness statements."

"I can help with the statements," she insisted, her stubborn streak rising up.

"And have the DA contest them later, saying the officer doing the questioning was unfit for duty? I don't think so."

"Fine." Frustrated with him, herself and the drunken fool who'd started the whole thing, she stalked over to an empty table and sat down to wait for the medics to check her over. How the heck was she going to prove herself to the department when her first shift ended up with her on the sidelines, watching the action?

* * *

Ryan tried to be patient as he dealt with the scared patrons who had witnessed the scene, but all he really wanted was to be by Jessica's side. She'd taken a hard hit, and despite her protests that she was fine, he was going to worry until a medical professional gave her the all clear. Seeing her pass out had rattled him more than any bad guy could. And yet now he was dealing with the grunt work while a team of medics hovered over her. Keeping one eye on them, and her, he tried to record every detail the woman in front of him was offering.

"He must have been sitting at the bar when we got here, because I don't remember him coming in. Of course, why would I? I was so busy telling Fred here about the deal I got on my new watch." She waved her wrist under his nose, as if somehow seeing the timepiece would clear everything up. Thankfully her husband, the aforementioned Fred, had been a bit more to the point with his statement. "But anyway, one minute I'm explaining about the percent off, and the extra coupons I had, and the next minute that man was pushing past our table, yelling about some lady named Doreen." She shook her head. "I think he was drunk. No good comes of strong drink, that's what my daddy told me. He was a preacher you know."

Ryan did know, because she'd mentioned it already. Along with the profession of her husband, where she'd gone to school and what she'd thought of her fish sandwich—too dry. "Did you see him attack the other deputy, ma'am?"

"Oh, no. I didn't see that, I'm afraid. I was facing Fred, and letting him know what I thought of men who drink. Thankfully Fred has never touched a drop."

Fred must be a saint, to deal with his wife's endlessly wagging tongue totally sober. Ryan was at the point of wanting a shot of something himself after listening to her go off on a half-dozen tangents. At least now that she'd admitted to not seeing the incident he could finish the interview. He'd gotten plenty of information from her husband, as well as from a few of the other patrons and a very shaken up waitress.

Across the dining area the paramedics were finishing up with Jessica. He wanted to hear what they said for himself—no doubt she'd minimize any possible injuries in an attempt to act tough.

No, he corrected himself. Her toughness wasn't an act, it was who she was. She'd proven that when she took on an armed man twice her size.

Handing the witness his card he strode over to where the medics were packing up their equipment. "How is she?"

"Her reflexes are good, and her pupils are reactive and even, but her blood pressure's lower than it should be, especially given all the excitement. Could be nothing, but she needs to go in ASAP to rule out internal bleeding."

"Seriously?" Jessica frowned. "Couldn't the low blood pressure just be from not eating?"

The medic shrugged. "Maybe. But it could also be dropping because you're hemorrhaging internally. That dude was big, and if he knocked into your spleen just right he could have damaged it. A CT scan can tell for sure."

"She'll get the scan right away," Ryan assured him. Hell, had she been sitting here, bleeding internally, while he was over there interviewing Mrs. Talks Too Much?

"Good. As soon as the ambulance gets back we'll take her straight over to the hospital." Catching Jessica's angry look he added, "If that's okay with you, ma'am."

"Fine." Her shoulders slumped in resignation.

"Wait, what do you mean, she needs to wait for the ambulance? Isn't it down in the parking lot? You rode in on it."

"The other guy's condition was critical. He couldn't wait, and at the time your partner here was still saying she didn't need medical attention. So they took him in and I stayed behind to check her over. They're sending the other unit, or if that one is already busy they'll bring the first one back after they unload."

Forget that. He wasn't going to wait however long that was going to take. "I'll drive her myself."

Jessica looked up, startled. "What about the witness statements?"

"I got what I need." This wasn't the movies where no one could leave until they had all spoken to a cop; the statements he'd gotten would have to do. He wasn't going to let her bleed to death for the sake of one more person's eyewitness account.

As if realizing she wasn't going to win this one, she got up and followed him, only glaring when he took her arm to help her down the stairs. Thankfully she didn't protest beyond that.

At the bottom he held out his hand for the keys, and he considered it a sign of how shaken she was that she handed them over without argument. But the cooperation didn't last long. They were barely onto the main road when she gave him a hopeful look.

"I don't suppose I could convince you to just take me home, huh? Forget all this happened?"

"No." His lips tightened as he pressed the gas pedal down further.

"I didn't think so." She slouched against the

door, arms tucked around herself. "I really do feel fine now."

"I'm happy to hear it. And I'll be even happier when someone with a medical degree agrees." He already felt guilty about their one-night stand, he wouldn't be able to live with himself if he took her home when she needed medical attention. His conscience could only handle so much.

Hospitals always smelled the same, like fear and antiseptic. Jessica tried to breathe through her mouth to avoid the harsh scent that was upsetting her stomach all over again.

"You okay? Are you feeling short of breath?" Ryan looked at her with concern edging on panic. "Maybe I should go get the nurse."

Jessica sighed and went back to breathing through her nose. This was bad enough without Ryan hovering over her. "I'm fine. But I think I'd rather be alone right now."

"Are you sure? If you have a head injury it would be better if you have someone with you."

"Ryan, I don't have a head injury. And any minute now they may need me to undress to get in one of those stupid hospital gowns, and I'd rather not have an audience." Even if he'd seen her in less before. Something she couldn't think about right now.

"Fine. I'll be right in the waiting room, if you need me."

"You don't need to do that. I'll be all right, and I can call someone to pick me up when they're done poking and prodding."

He narrowed his eyes. "I'll be in the waiting room."

"Fine. Suit yourself." At least he'd be out of her hair. And really, she didn't want to have to call her mom or brother to pick her up—it would mean having to admit she'd been injured her very first night as a deputy. Her mother would worry herself to death and her brother would say I told you so, and she'd never live any of it down. Better Ryan's version of overprotective than theirs.

Once he left she settled back onto the single chair in the curtained-off area they'd stuck her in. She was probably supposed to be on the hospital bed, but that would mean acknowledging she was a patient. No thank you. She'd sit in a chair until they told her otherwise.

"Miss?" A tall woman with gray hair cut in a stylish bob stepped in, her scrubs marking her as one of the medical staff. "I'm Elsie, one of the nurses. How are you feeling?"

Jessica found herself smiling despite herself. The nurse gave off a vibe of compassion and kindness that was hard to resist. Or maybe her defenses were just weak after the last hour. "I'm feeling fine, really. I'd just like to get this over with so I can leave."

"Well, I'll do my best to make things quick. You came on a good night. Other than the man who attacked you we haven't had a lot of activity."

"You heard about that, huh?"

"Oh, yes. Everyone's talking about the brave young woman who single-handedly saved Pete's Crab Shack from an angry drunk. You're something of the hero."

Jessica winced. She'd hoped to hide the whole debacle from her family, but if Elsie was right about how quickly word was spreading, then the story would be all over town before the sun was up. And although the nurse might think she was a hero, she doubted her brother or the rest of the department would see it that way. After all, heroes didn't pass out and end up in the emergency room.

Nothing to be done about it now, other than submit to yet another series of questions about her health—good, her eating habits—not so good, her menstrual cycle—irregular, and any previous surgeries—none. Then she'd been asked to change into one of those horrid gowns, and escorted down the hall where she dutifully peed in a cup. No doubt they would check her urine for drugs. That was standard with work-related accidents, wasn't it? No worries there, she didn't even like the way cold medicine made her feel, let alone anything stronger.

Finally, after giving what seemed like most of her blood for whatever lab tests they needed to run, a doctor came in. Middle-aged, with weathered skin that spoke of some kind of outdoor hobby, he had her climb up on the dreaded hospital bed for an exam. After finding every sore spot and bruise with his deft fingers he shined a light in her eyes, thumped on her knees and left, promising to be back with results as soon as he could.

Alone at last, she tried to concentrate on a plan to repair her reputation in the department. She'd spent her time at the academy learning to project a strong, cool, confident persona, and now she was going to be the girl who fainted at the sight of blood. Which made no sense, because she'd never been bothered by that kind of thing before. It had to just be the stress about the first day on a new job, and the lack of food in her system. But that wouldn't matter to those looking for a reason to discredit a woman in law enforcement.

At least thinking about her job problems was better than worrying about the possibility of internal bleeding. She didn't *feel* like she was hemorrhaging anywhere, but how would she know? Did a spleen injury hurt, like a cut finger, or would she just get weaker and weaker until she passed out again, maybe for good this time? A shiver of fear wormed its way in, making her wish she hadn't been left quite so alone. Maybe she should call her brother after all. He'd yell at her, but fighting with him beat sitting around with nothing to do but worry about dying.

A rustle startled her out of her thoughts, and she turned to see Ryan poking his head around the curtain that surrounded her bed. His eyes were shut, and he looked ridiculous. Ridiculous and wonderful.

"Hey, are you decent? I know you said you wanted to be alone but the captain was asking if there was any news, and the nurses won't tell me anything."

She checked that the flimsy hospital gown covered everything worth covering, and called to him. "Come on in—and you can open your eyes. I'm just waiting for the lab results, and there was talk of doing some kind of scan, depending on what they find. It could be a while."

"You're sure?"

"Yeah." Sitting alone had lost its appeal. Any distraction was better than wondering what might be wrong.

As if reading her mind, he bypassed the chair and sat down next to her on the bed, far enough away for modesty's sake but close enough for moral support.

A minute later, the doctor returned, a clipboard in his hand. He stopped when he saw Ryan. "I didn't realize you had a visitor. Perhaps, sir, I could ask you to step out for a minute? For the patient's privacy?"

Ryan started to stand but Jessica put a hand on his arm, stopping him. "He might as well stay." If she was going to get bad news, she didn't want to be alone. "He's my partner, he needs to know what my situation is, medically, for us to work together." That sounded better than just saying she was scared, right?

"If you're sure." He glanced down at the paperwork again, and then cleared his throat. "The good news is, we don't think there is any internal bleeding."

"You don't *think*?" Ryan interrupted. "Shouldn't you be sure? Isn't that what the CT scan was for?"

The doctor raised an eyebrow, and continued. "As I was saying, we don't think there is any internal bleeding based on the blood work we did, and the physical exam. No tenderness was noted, and her red blood count is excellent, as are her platelets. A CT scan would give more definitive information, of course, but I'm afraid that is contraindicated during pregnancy."

"Wait, what? I'm not pregnant."

Turning the clipboard to face her, the doctor pointed out a line of test results where the word *positive* had been circled. "Actually, Miss Santiago, according to your this, you are."

Chapter Four

Jessica's first reaction was to laugh, the sound slightly hysterical even to her own ears. "Pregnant? You must be kidding. Or you got the samples mixed up. Or something." The last word came out strangled, as fear tightened its grip on her body.

His eyes softened, and he lowered his voice. "I'm afraid not. I'm sorry, I thought you already knew. From the level of hormones detected you are far enough along that you should have missed at least one period by now."

Pregnant? Period? She was as fluent in English as she was in her mother's native Spanish, but somehow the words just refused to make sense.

But the doctor seemed to be waiting for a response of some sort, so she answered on autopilot. "I have irregular cycles. I often skip a few months. It runs in the family."

"And you aren't on birth control?"

"I haven't needed it." She blushed. Obviously she *had* needed it, at least that one time. But they'd used a condom. Tequila or not, she remembered that much clearly.

Ryan was obviously thinking along the same lines. "But we used protection." His face had gone slightly white under the dark stubble that lined his jaw.

The doctor shot an amused glance to Ryan before clearing his throat. "Oh, I see. Well then, as I'm sure you know, condoms are not one hundred percent effective. Of course, nothing is."

Ryan nodded, his jaw clenched so tight she was afraid he might break a tooth.

"The perp landed right on my abdomen. Do you think the baby—"

"He or she is probably fine. The human body is designed to protect the fetus. But to be safe, I'd like to do an ultrasound. We can make sure everything is as it should be, and take some measurements that will give us a more accurate understanding of how far along you are."

"Eight weeks."

Ryan turned a startled look her way, and the Doctor looked up from his paperwork. "I'm sorry, I thought you said you didn't know you were pregnant?"

"I don't. I mean I didn't. But it's been two months since graduation, and there was only the one time…" She blushed. The doctor didn't need the details of her sex life, or the lack there of. Neither did Ryan, for that matter. Other than the part he'd participated in, of course.

"I'd still like to do the ultrasound."

She nodded, too shell-shocked to form actual words.

"I'll just get the equipment then," he said, leaving her alone again with Ryan. Standing against the wall, his hands held rigidly at his sides, he looked straight ahead, avoiding her gaze.

"I didn't know." Somehow it seemed important he understand that. Not that it changed anything.

"So I heard."

Anger bubbled to the surface, working its way past the shock and terror that had gripped her. She embraced it, using its heat to chase off the chill of fear. "It's true. I certainly didn't plan for this to happen. And I didn't get into this situation on my own."

"That's not what I meant. Or maybe it is—hell, I don't know what I meant." He shoved a hand through his hair, frustration radiating off him so strongly she could practically feel it on her skin.

The curtain rustled, signaling the return of the doctor, this time pushing what must be the ultrasound machine.

"If you could just lie down, we'll take a peek."

"Oh, right. Sorry." She carefully positioned herself on the crinkly paper–covered bed, carefully covering her lower body with the flimsy sheet before pulling her gown up to expose her stomach. Modesty at this point might be along the lines of closing the barn door after the horse had bolted, but she didn't care. She was holding on to her dignity by her fingernails right now and would take what comfort she could.

"Dad, you'll need to come closer if you want to see the monitor."

Ryan visibly startled at the familial term, and shook his head.

Jessica's stomach clenched. He didn't want to see the baby. Probably didn't want to be involved with the pregnancy or the baby at all. Why would he? She wasn't anything to him, they barely knew each other. Great sex and a shared commitment to the law wasn't enough to build a relationship on, let alone a family.

Cold jelly, wet and slippery on her stomach, dragged her from her thoughts. Once she was sufficiently covered in the slimy stuff the doctor placed a probe on her abdomen, pressing down against her flesh.

She had to strain her neck to see the monitor, but even staring right at it she wasn't sure what she was seeing. Nothing on the screen looked remotely like a baby. She'd thought maybe some instinct would guide her eye…but so far, no such luck. She'd known about the pregnancy for only a few minutes, and she already felt like a bad mother. Frustrated, she squinted at the black-and-white squiggles, unwilling to broadcast her ineptness by asking for help. It was bad enough she'd had to admit she didn't know she'd been pregnant, she wasn't going to give the doctor, or Ryan, any more reason to doubt her capabilities to handle this pregnancy. Shouldn't she be able identify her own baby when looking right at it?

As if sensing her confusion, the doctor smiled, the tired lines around his eyes softening. "See that dark area? That's your uterus. And this white spot that looks a bit like a peanut? That's your baby."

Her breath caught in her throat. Her baby.

"And that flickering there? What's that?" Ryan's deep voice caught her off guard. He'd come closer to see, despite his earlier refusal.

"That's the heartbeat. Give me a second and I'll let you hear it."

Jessica raised her eyes to meet Ryan's as a steady *thump thump* filled the room. Through the unshed tears blurring her vision she saw him swallow hard.

"One hundred and seventy beats per minute."

"Is that good?" she asked.

"It is. In fact, everything looks perfect. Seems baby is none the worse for wear after your incident."

"Perfect." She repeated the doctor's word, and knew he was wrong. Not that she wasn't grateful the baby was okay. She was. But the situation was far from perfect. In fact, her life was now about as messed up as it could be. And she had no idea what to do about it.

At least a dozen different emotions had worked their way through Ryan in the last ten minutes. Ever since he heard the word pregnant. But now, looking at that little flickering light on the monitor, there was only one feeling filling him from top to bottom.

Love.

Not for Jessica, of course. As much as it would make things simpler if they were a happy, devoted couple, the truth was they were still in the lust phase. But he did feel love, stronger than he'd known was possible, for the little baby growing inside of her. He'd tried to keep his cool, to stay detached and let Jessica deal with things before shoving his way into matters, but when the doctor had pointed out the baby on the screen he'd wanted—no, needed—to see. And from the second he'd watched that little heart pumping away, fighting for life, he'd fallen head over heels.

Fatherhood hadn't been in his plans, not anytime soon anyway, but there was no denying the instant sense of connection he'd felt. And then the crushing weight of responsibility. He knew more than most how much influence a father had on a child. He wasn't even close to ready for that, but there was no way he would turn his back on his own flesh and blood.

And he could see in Jessica's eyes that she feared just that. No doubt a surprise pregnancy was scary for any woman, but to find out like this, after such a shock, had to be terrifying.

Not that she'd show it. That was one thing he did know about her—she didn't back down from a challenge. The way she'd taken on the perp tonight showed that. But right now her eyes were misting over and he knew that he'd caused whatever stress and anxiety she was feeling. If he'd kept his hands off her…

But he hadn't. And now he needed to find a way to make it right by her. And by their child.

Taking her hand where it lay on the hospital bed, looking nearly as white as the sheet she'd covered herself with, he squeezed, hoping to communicate to her that he'd find a way to fix things. It wasn't much, but it was a start.

He tried not to let her soft skin distract him as he listened to information the doctor was giving on prenatal vitamins, due dates and the need to stay hydrated and eat more frequently. Finally the doctor finished, leaving a referral to a local ob-gyn, a handout on the prenatal classes offered at the hospital and a warning for Jessica to take it easy for the rest of the night.

Now alone with her in the tiny curtained room, the silence between them stretched awkwardly, broken only by the beeping of equipment and the hushed tones of the staff as they tended to other patients nearby. Wordlessly, Jessica swiped at the gel left on her stomach with a tissue. He found himself watching, looking for some sign of the pregnancy on her still-flat abdomen.

"Do you mind?"

"What?"

"I need to get dressed. Alone."

"Right." He cleared his throat. "I'll just wait outside."

He paced the green-and-white-tiled corridor while she dressed, racking his brain for a way to make this turn out right. But when she emerged in a pair of borrowed scrubs, her bloody clothes bagged as evidence, he was still too shell-shocked to think clearly.

"Are you okay?" he asked, wincing at the trite words. But it wasn't like he had better ones. *Was* there a right thing to say to a fellow officer of the law that you just happened to have accidentally impregnated?

"Okay?" The brittleness of her voice ripped at his conscience, scraping away any pretense of normality. "Nothing about this is okay. But don't worry, I'll handle it."

"What do you mean, you'll handle it? This is as much my problem as it is yours."

"Problem? That's what you think I am? What this baby is? A *problem*? Thanks, but no thanks. I don't need your help."

Crap. He was making things worse, which— given how bad things had been even before he opened his mouth—was pretty impressive. Stepping in front of her, blocking her path to the door, he tried again. "I didn't mean you were a problem. Or the baby. I just meant that I know this is a tough situation and I want to help. I want to do my part."

"Your part? What does that even mean? Are you going to carry the baby? Are you going to get morning sickness for me, or give birth? Are you going to have to face the commander and explain why you're going to need maternity leave after less than a year on the job? Are you going to have to juggle nursing and pumping and working?"

Her eyes filled again and he found himself wishing he had an answer that would make things all right. But he didn't. "No, you're right. I can't do those things for you. But I do want to help. Just tell me what to do, what you need."

"Honestly Ryan, I'm not trying to be difficult, but there's nothing you can do right now. In fact, what I really need is for you to get the hell out of my way."

Jessica had been equal parts surprised and relieved when Ryan had let her leave the hospital without any further issues. She was even feeling the tiniest bit guilty over the way she'd treated him. But dammit, she was tired, and hungry and sore all over. Add in her entire life being turned upside down and she was past the point of being polite. Hell, she was almost past the point of being coherent.

A strange punch-drunk sensation came over her as she climbed into the cab the front desk had called for her. Riding back with Ryan was out of the question, and so was calling her family. Which meant she'd just been giving the biggest news of her life and had no one to tell but an overweight taxi driver who smelled of stale cigarette smoke and cheap aftershave.

"I'm pregnant."

"Huh?"

She giggled, the absurdity of the night catching up with her. The laugh held more hysteria than amusement—but laughing was still better than crying. "I'm pregnant. And I barely know the father. Oh, and I might lose my job." Her chest tightened on that last bit, but after the adrenaline rush at the bar and then the news of the pregnancy it was like she had run out of fight-or-flight hormones. She just didn't have any more panic in her. Not tonight.

"Well, um, congratulations. And, I'm sorry. Er…"

She laughed again, this time at his flabbergasted expression, letting the tension of the last few hours leak out with each breath, until she felt as limp as a deflated balloon. No doubt Mister Smoky upfront thought she was a lunatic, but that was okay. The reputation she'd worked so hard to build was about to be destroyed, so what did the opinion of one cab driver matter?

Minutes later she was on her own front steps, or rather her mother's front steps. She was scheduled to move into her own apartment on the first of the month. It was a dingy little place in the worst part of town, but it was all she could afford on her new salary. She'd promised herself she'd find a better place once she'd saved up some money, but with the baby coming who knew when that would be.

The irony was that she had plenty of money sitting in the bank, an inheritance from her grandmother. It was in a trust fund that was supposed to transfer to her after the birth of her first child, or on her thirtieth birthday, whichever came first. Except dear old grandma had been a devout Catholic, and had specified that if the baby came first, Jessica had to be married to get the money. Babies born out of wedlock were not an option as far as Grams was concerned.

Jessica pushed those thoughts aside. She was too tired and too hungry to figure anything out right now. As if on cue her stomach grumbled, probably triggered by the incredible aroma seeping through her front door.

Free food was definitely the biggest perk of living at home. Unfortunately, her mother's home-cooked dishes came with a heaping side of motherly advice and unlimited refills of guilt. If you looked up *overprotective* in the dictionary there was a picture of her mother. Jessica wasn't sure if it was worse for her because she was the only girl, or because she was the youngest, or because her brother, Alex, now had his own family, but whatever the reason, it had gotten worse in the past year or two. Of course, joining the sheriff's department had just added fuel to her mother's worries.

And now she had to tell her mom she'd ended up in the hospital on her first day in uniform. That wasn't going to go over well.

At all.

And the pregnancy? That news would keep until after this round of maternal guilt was over. One crisis at a time.

Hoping to delay the inevitable at least long enough to change into her own clothes, she inched the door open as silently as possible, easing it closed behind her. She made it all of three feet down the hall before her mother, using whatever superpowers mothers had, sensed her presence.

"Jessica, is that you?"

"*Si*, Mama."

"Well, come here so I can talk to you without yelling across the house."

Knowing it was useless to argue, she turned back toward her mother's small but cheery kitchen. "I didn't expect you so early, are you on a dinner break? Just let me finish up these dishes and I will fix you up a plate of food."

"I'm home for the night. There was a bit of an incident…"

Her mother spun around, her hands dripping

dish suds onto the tile and her eyes filled with fear. "An incident? *Dios mio*, what happened? Where are your clothes—your uniform? Did you quit?"

Jessica couldn't help but detect the note of hope in that last question, layered on top of the thicker layer of concern.

"No, I didn't quit. I was involved in an arrest and a man was injured. There was a lot of blood—his, not mine—so I had to put on clean clothes."

"But those are scrubs, from a hospital."

Jessica sighed. Obviously her mother wasn't going to let her get away without telling her the full truth. Or at least something close to it. "I'm fine. Really, I am. But during the arrest the man fell on me. They took me to the hospital to make sure I was okay. Which I am," she insisted as firmly as she could.

"And that is all that happened?"

Jessica squirmed under her mother's steady stare. It was the same look her mom had given her when she was five years old and had a broken the neighbor's planter. She'd never been able to hold out under that stare. "I may also have passed out. But just for a minute. I guess I get squeamish at the sight of blood."

"Since when?"

Jessica ignored the question. "Or, the paramedics said it could be because I hadn't eaten today. I guess I have to be better about that."

Her mother took the bait. "Well that's the truth. I've been telling you that for a long time. The way you run around on nothing but fast food and candy bars, it's no wonder you had a problem. Why don't you sit down and I'll fix you up something."

Jessica took a deep breath and sat at the table, grateful for the reprieve. Eventually she was going to have to tell her mother about the pregnancy, but not tonight. There was no way she was up to weathering that particular storm right now. First she would sleep. Everything else could wait until morning.

Chapter Five

Ryan spent the rest of his first shift with the Paradise sheriff's department riding a desk. It seemed no one was eager to send the rookie back out on the street after he let his partner land in the hospital. Besides, he had more than enough paperwork to keep himself busy, or "out of trouble" as the sergeant had said. Unfortunately, neither the stack of documentation he was working through nor the sergeant's obvious annoyance was enough to keep his mind off the scene at the hospital.

Funny, a few hours ago his biggest concerns had been making a good impression on the senior officers and staying awake for the graveyard shift. Those fears were only a few hours old, but they seemed like something from another lifetime.

Part of him was panicking, totally freaking out over the idea of a baby. Like most young single guys raising a kid wasn't on his top ten list of things to do. At least not for another decade, give or take. Just the idea would be laughable if it wasn't so panic inducing.

But layered beneath the terror was a niggle of excitement. A small thread of hope rising up through the fear.

Family was everything—he'd always believed that. It was one of the reasons he was so determined to be a cop, to carry on his father's legacy. And now there would be another generation, a new O'Sullivan to carry on the family name.

Unless Jessica wanted the baby to have her last name.

That was a very real possibility. They weren't married, they weren't even a couple. Heck, after tonight they probably wouldn't even be partnered together again. They were coworkers who had had a fling. A one-night stand.

Even as he thought it, he rejected the term. They may have been intimate only once, but it hadn't been just the whim of a moment. He'd been drawn to her since the first time he laid on eyes on her. She had a magnetism, an intensity to her that outshined the more flirtatious, forward women he'd known. And now, knowing she carried his child, the pull was only stronger.

Of course, she had given no indication she felt the same way toward him. In fact, her leaving so quickly without any contact information or even a goodbye made it pretty clear that she didn't. And right now his feelings for her needed to take a back seat while they figured out how to be parents together.

The first step would be getting Jessica to talk to him. After the way he'd put his foot in his mouth when they'd last spoken, that was going to be difficult. Somehow, he had to convince her that as surprised and scared as he was he was also looking forward to the baby, and wanted to be involved.

He was still pondering how to do that when he clocked out in the wee hours of the morning. By all rights he should be exhausted but instead he was on edge, too wired to head home and sleep. So instead of turning toward his apartment, he headed east, to where the land and the sea met.

He parked his car by one of the access stairways and got out, breathing in the clean salt-tanged air. Sand crunched under his feet as he walked, his steps taking him up and over the dunes to the beach beyond. There he stared out at the moon reflecting on the glittering waves and searched for the peace that the ocean always brought him. When his dad had died, when he and his stepfather were arguing, when he felt lost and wasn't sure how he was going to find a way forward, he had always found solace at the beach. Tonight though, even the waves and the ocean breeze couldn't wash away the riot of emotion surging through him.

Like many times before, he found himself wishing he had his father to talk to. His dad had been a simple man in many ways, but full of wisdom. He told it like it was, and that kind of directness was exactly what Ryan needed right now.

"Dad, I've made a mess of things. But I'm going to try to fix them."

Although maybe it was better his father wasn't here to see how badly he'd screwed up. From an early age his father had taught him to respect women, and be responsible when it came to sex. Sure, they used protection. But like the doctor said, condoms weren't one hundred percent effective. Thinking back, he couldn't remember if he had checked the expiration date. He wasn't sure how old the box had been—he'd been too busy studying to have many occasions to use them.

He should have checked.

He should have asked if she was on birth control.

And he should have found a way to keep in touch with her after that night.

What would've happened if he hadn't come to Paradise? If his buddy hadn't needed to be in Miami to help take care of a sick relative? Would he even know about the pregnancy? Would Jessica have known how to find him to tell him? Would she have even bothered to try?

The thought that he might have had a child and never known about it made him sick to his stomach. That wasn't the kind of guy he wanted to be. But proving himself to Jessica was going to be an uphill battle. He would do it though. He would find a way to be the man that his father would want him to be. The man he wanted himself to be. A man worthy of her.

The morning dawned too early and too bright, forcing Jessica to shade her eyes against the harsh rays shining through her window as she fumbled for the snooze button. Ten more minutes, then she'd get up. Burrowing back down into the covers she tried to find a comfortable position on the lumpy sleeper sofa.

Two weeks. Fourteen days until her new apartment would be ready. Until then she was stuck sleeping on the pull-out couch in her mother's sewing room. The lumpy mattress was better than nothing, and she should be grateful for the free rent, but the situation was seriously lacking in many ways. It had been tolerable for quick visits home during college, but now that she was actually living in Paradise full time she needed her own space, and some distance from her well meaning but ever-present mother.

As if to underscore that thought, there was a knock on the door. "Jessica, you have a visitor. *Un muy guapo* visitor."

Jessica's stomach did a quick somersault—not from morning sickness this time, just plain old nerves. The only person who would be visiting her this early was Ryan. And yeah, he was handsome, but he was the last person she wanted to see.

Another knock. "Jessica, it isn't polite to keep a man waiting."

Lovely. Now her mother wanted to play cupid. Yeah, it was a little too late for that. She and Ryan had skipped the boyfriend and girlfriend phase and gone straight to the awkward former fling phase. And mom wasn't going to be happy about that, although the promise of a new grandchild would probably mollify her somewhat. Her mom had dreamed of Jessica's wedding since before she'd even been born. It had gotten only worse since her brother, Alex, had married and started a family.

Jessica was happy for her brother, but marriage

was the last thing she was looking for. As the baby of the family she'd had other people trying to make her decisions for her whole life. It was only when she'd left for college that she had finally started to feel free of the well-intentioned but smothering love of her family. She'd gotten a taste of independence, and she liked it.

She might be living on her mom's couch, but that didn't mean she had to let those old patterns reassert themselves.

She groaned as she threw on a pair of sweatpants and an old football jersey, her sleep-heavy body slow to cooperate.

First coffee. The paperwork from the hospital had said that two cups a day was safe—and she badly needed one of them right now.

Then Ryan.

Then her mother.

And then, she had to go back to work and face all the questions that would arise there.

Today was not going to be a good day.

Ryan was waiting for her in the living room, seated on the floral couch across from her mother's favorite chair. Her mother held court from that chair as much as any queen on her throne. A true matriarch who ruled over her family with a benevolent but firm hand.

"There you are, Jessica. I was just asking Ryan to stay for breakfast."

"Mom, I'm sure Ryan is too busy to stay. We just need to discuss some paperwork issues, isn't that right Ryan?"

Ryan turned a startled glance her way at the lie, then nodded in agreement. "Um…that's right. Paperwork. I just need Jessica's signature on a few of the reports from last night." Jessica let out a relieved breath. The story probably wouldn't hold her mother off for long, but it would give her at least a little breathing room. She'd deal with one difficult person at a time. "Ryan, why don't I grab us each a cup of coffee and I'll meet you on the front porch. We can look over things out there."

"Sounds good," he said, rising. "It was nice to meet you, Mrs. Santiago."

Her mother looked from one to the other, one eyebrow raised. Oh yeah, she knew there was more going on than met the eye, but at least she was too polite to say so in front of a guest. No doubt the questions would come fast and furious once Ryan had left.

"The pleasure was mine. It's always nice to meet one of Jessica's friends. Perhaps you can come by another time and stay for dinner. Jessica is a fantastic cook."

Jessica rolled her eyes at her mother's shameless and fallacious attempt at matchmaking. "I'll just be a minute."

She left Ryan to show himself back out to the porch and headed for the kitchen and the coffee. Avoiding her mother's eyes, she focused on loading a tray with two steaming mugs of the rich Cuban brew as well as a bowl of sugar and a small carton of cream.

"Would you like me to bring you out some pastries?" her mother asked, no doubt hoping to eavesdrop on their conversation. Her mom had better instincts than any private investigator, a trait that had annoyed Jessica to no end as a teenager.

"No thanks, Mom. I'll eat something when I come back in."

It was only May, but stepping outside was like stepping into a sauna. It had rained briefly at some point—not enough to cool things off, just enough to send the humidity sky high, making it feel like even the air was sweating.

But there was a fan to stir up a breeze, and she'd rather be outside with the privacy than in the air-conditioning with her mother attempting to overhear.

Making sure the heavy front door was securely closed behind her, she set the tray down on the small glass top patio table and motioned for Ryan to help himself.

Once he had fixed his coffee to his liking she took her own mug and cradled it. She didn't need the added beverage's heat given the weather, but she did need the caffeine. And on the topic of things she needed, she could also use a miracle. Some way forward that didn't involve living on her mother's couch, losing her job or being broke for the rest of her life.

Needing to break the awkward silence, and to take her mind off how good he looked despite probably having gotten even less sleep than she had, she decided to clear the air. "Thanks for playing along. I haven't told my mother yet—though I'm sure I will soon. Please don't think she was implying that you have any kind of responsibility toward me. Just so you know, I don't expect anything from you. I know this was an accident, and I don't blame you. So if you are here to ease your conscience you don't need to bother. I've got things covered."

Ryan blinked once, then took another slow sip of coffee before setting down his mug. "That was a great speech. How long did it take you to come up with it?"

Jessica flushed. "It's not a speech. It's the truth." He didn't need to know that she'd spent several hours last night putting the words together.

"Well I've got a speech of my own," Ryan said, easing from his chair onto one knee.

"Jessica Santiago, will you marry me?"

Chapter Six

Ryan waited in silence as Jessica's mouth hung open in shock. Part of him was enjoying seeing the always-composed Jessica finally rendered speechless. Another part of him was taut with anxiety, unsure how she was going to answer. And all of him was busy taking in how gorgeous she looked.

Even in a ratty shirt two sizes too big, with her hair piled on her head in a messy knot, she was spellbinding. He liked seeing her all tousled and half awake. He'd missed out on that after their one night together, when she'd snuck out while he was still sleeping, and he intended to make up for it.

And he would, if she would agree to his plan.

She *had* to agree, it was the only thing that made sense. At least that was what he had decided around 4:00 a.m., after evaluating every possible scenario. He just needed to find the right way to convince her.

"Well, are you going to say anything?"

She shook her head, her eyes wide and dilated in confusion. "Is this some kind of sick joke? Because it isn't funny."

"It's not a joke. I'm serious. You and I both know what it is like to grow up in a single-parent household. I want to give our child better than that, and I believe you do too."

"We can't get married just because we're having a child. This isn't the 1950s."

Maybe not, but that wasn't his only reason. Of course if she wasn't pregnant he wouldn't be ready to propose, but he had been captivated with her since they met, which was why it was no hardship to give up his spot in Miami for a friend. He'd been more than happy to have an excuse to see Jessica again. And late at night, when he couldn't sleep, he thought of her. But he knew her well enough to know she didn't want to hear any of that. If he claimed he had feelings for her, she'd say he was being ridiculous, and she would probably be right. So he left all that out and tried to appeal to her logic. "You have to agree that there would be benefits. First of all housing. Unless you were planning on raising the baby here?"

A look of horror crossed her face. "Definitely not. I love my mom, but we tolerate each other best in small doses. I'm not sure we would both survive if I stayed here long-term." She took another sip of her coffee, as if the very thought had left a bad taste in her mouth. "But I don't see why that means I should move in with you. I have my own apartment lined up—my lease starts in a few weeks."

"No offense, but I know how big of a place a rookie deputy can afford."

"Newsflash—you make the same salary I do. What makes you think your place is any better than the one I'm moving into?"

"Because I'm not renting an apartment. I had a little money set aside from my dad's life insurance and I used it for a down payment on a cottage on the other side of town. It needs work, but it has good bones, and the price was right. I'm fixing it up a little at a time, and I can more than cover the mortgage on just my salary."

"I don't need you to pay my way. I can take care of myself." Jessica's eyes sparked with anger, and darned if he didn't find the sight sexy as hell. But if he told her that, she'd probably kick his ass.

"Look, I'm not disputing that you'd find a way to handle things on your own. But this isn't just about you. When that baby comes your pride isn't going to pay for a playpen or for diapers. Admit it, you're going to need help."

"Maybe." He could tell from her frown that she hated admitting even that. "But there is such a thing as child support. If you are so all-fired determined to help you can write a check."

"And if that is all you will accept, then I will. But I want to do more. I think our child deserves more. I want to be there for the first kick. I want to make midnight runs for ice cream cravings. I want to be there for those middle-of-the-night feedings. I want to change diapers and give baths. I want to be a father to this baby, and in order to do that as fully as I'd like to, I want to be a partner to you."

Her eyes widened at that last part. "Please. You aren't going to try and convince me that you're in love with me and that we will just be one big happy family, are you? I'd have thought you of all people would have known the difference between sex and romance. Or do you propose to all your one-night stands?"

He winced, her words arrowing in on the parts of himself he was least comfortable with. "No, I don't. And I'm not going to lie and say I'm in love with you. But being with you was a hell of a lot more than just scratching an itch. Admit it,

Jessica, there's something between us, something that you can't deny."

Jessica allowed herself the space of a single heartbeat before answering. Any longer and she might let his pretty words and all the practical benefits of marriage—including the chance at getting her hands on her trust fund—overtake her good sense. "I'm sorry, Ryan, but I can't tell you what you want to hear. Whatever you think you feel for me… It's not real." Strange, how the words tasted like a lie on her tongue.

Unwilling to think about why, she forced a smile. "It's very sweet, though, for you to go to all this trouble. Very chivalrous. I don't suppose you have a white horse hidden somewhere, do you?"

If Ryan was frustrated by her refusal, he didn't show it. Despite the heat he remained cool and collected. "Fine. I had hoped that you felt something, like I did. And I'd hoped it could turn into more if we gave it a chance. But I won't push you on that. You have every right to your feelings."

She sighed, relief flooding through her body. She didn't need this to be any more awkward than it already was. Feelings would just make things messier. "Good. Then we agree we need to approach this from a purely logistical standpoint."

"I'm glad you said that. Because I have a plan B for you."

"And what is that?"

Pleased with the more reasonable turn to the conversation, Jessica took a deep drink from her coffee.

"A marriage of convenience."

Jessica sputtered, sweetened coffee spraying everywhere, burning her sinuses as she choked and coughed. "A what? Didn't those go out of style with arranged marriages and bodice ripper romance novels?"

"Hear me out. That's all I ask."

Dumbstruck, she nodded and wiped her face with the hem of her shirt. She couldn't imagine what on earth he was thinking, but at this point she had too much to lose to not at least listen.

"I've already mentioned the financial benefit as far as housing."

Cautiously she nodded.

"Living costs in general would be less. I know you say you can handle things, but we both know how tight a cop's budget is. In all honesty, child support will be a real stretch for me, on top of paying my own bills. I'll do it if we decide that's the best option," he hastened to add. "I'm not trying to shirk my responsibility. But the money will go a lot further if we consolidate households."

Somehow she never expected a proposal of marriage to include a discussion of consolidation. Even she was more romantic than that.

But he wasn't done yet.

"There is also the matter of insurance."

"Insurance?" She probably shouldn't even be engaging in this conversation, but maybe his foolishness was rubbing off on her.

"Health insurance."

"I've already got a policy. The same one as yours."

"I know. But what happens if you have complications and can't work? Or if you want to stay home after the baby is born?"

She held up a hand to stop him. "I *will* be going back to work." That part was nonnegotiable. She needed to know that she could support herself. She couldn't imagine giving up working entirely.

"That's fine. I'll support you in whatever you want to do. But there is always a chance that something could happen during the pregnancy. Besides, once the baby comes it will be less expensive to have one family policy."

She caught herself nodding. Surely she wasn't actually agreeing with him? But after the way she had passed out last night she couldn't deny that the pregnancy made her more vulnerable. She couldn't be sure what medical complications she might face—and that had her uneasy. She didn't like the feeling. "I kind of get what you are saying. That doesn't mean I agree, but I see where you're coming from. But this doesn't sound like a plan B. This sounds like the same plan you started out with, just with different reasons behind it. I'm not going to tie myself to someone until death do us part just for a better insurance rate." Even her inheritance wasn't enough to justify that kind of commitment. "Isn't there some saying, about not choosing a permanent solution to a temporary problem?"

Ryan leaned forward putting his elbows on his knees, his gaze intense. "I get that. But what if it wasn't a lifetime commitment? What if it was for a set duration?"

"Marriage doesn't work that way, Ryan."

"It could. If we wanted it to. I'm thinking a year. By then the baby will have been born and be old enough for daycare. You will have taken your maternity leave and you'll be back at work. And between now and then you can save up for a better place for you and the baby to live once we go our separate ways. It makes sense, Jessica. You know it does."

"A year?" That she was even considering his plan was a sign she needed her head examined. But as preposterous as his idea was, it did make a strange kind of sense. She didn't like the thought of living off someone else's dime, but if she saved all the money she would have spent on rent, then even if he changed his mind after a few months, she would have a decent financial cushion. And if they made it until the baby came, she'd get her inheritance money. Nothing in the will said she had to stay married…just be married when the baby was born.

And although she shouldn't care, it would be a lot easier to break the news of the pregnancy to her mother if she was also announcing an engagement. It would probably be better for her reputation at work and in the community as well. Even in this day and age an unwed mother faced a stigma.

She hated to think she'd be using Ryan for financial gain and respectability, but it *had* been his idea. He wouldn't have suggested it if he wasn't going to benefit too, right? He seemed sincere about wanting to be actively involved as a father. Did she really have the right to deny him that? It was his baby too.

It was hard to believe that she was contemplating saying yes, but then again the last twenty-four hours had all been pretty surreal. Her world had turned upside down and all the rules had changed. Her new life was going to require her to step outside her comfort zone.

It would be hard to give up her plans of living alone, the independent life she had fought for, even if it was just temporary. But there was one thing she would not compromise on.

"We're going to need to talk about sex."

Ryan's body stirred even as his brain realized he probably wouldn't like where this was going. "What about it?"

"We aren't going to be having it. Sex, I mean. If this is going to be a marriage in name only then it can't get physical. I don't want to complicate things."

"Honey, I'd say the physical end of things is the least complicated part of our relationship. And it's not like you can get any more pregnant."

"I'm serious. If I agree to do this, and I'm not saying I will, but if I do, I need you to respect my boundaries."

"What kind of boundaries? Other than no sex."

"I want my own bank account. I don't want to combine finances."

"Fine." He nodded and leaned back in his chair, stretching his legs out in front of him. He had no issue with her having her own money. He also planned to open a separate savings account for the baby, for college expenses or anything else he or she needed.

"I get to make my own decisions. Just because we sign some papers doesn't mean you get to tell me what to do, or how to live."

"Of course not." Jessica was far from being a damsel in distress or a shrinking violet in need of someone to take charge. His ego might like to pretend he was rescuing her, but she was more than capable of handling things without him. He just didn't want her to need to. "I'm not trying to take over your life, Jessica. I just want to make things easier for you and the baby. Anything else?"

She paused, tapping one finger on the table, before finally answering. "I don't think so."

"Then I'd like to propose one amendment to your list of conditions."

"I'm not backing down on the no sex rule," she warned, her tone firm.

He smiled. "How about no sex unless you ask for it? I wouldn't want you to be locked into something you might regret later."

She rolled her eyes. "I'm not going to ask for it."

"I don't know, I've heard that pregnant women often get very…how shall we say…amorous. It's the hormones."

She raised an eyebrow. "And you heard this where, exactly? Doesn't seem like the kind of trivia you'd pick up in the locker room at the gym."

"Um…" He ducked his head and looked down at the worn but clean boards that made up the porch floor. "It was on a reality show…one of the ones about rich housewives…" He scratched his neck.

Her giggle had him looking up again. She was a goddess when she laughed, and he'd happily embarrass himself more often if it meant seeing her like this.

"I don't think that counts as a reliable source."

"Maybe not, but aside from all that, I seem to remember that you enjoyed our night together." He kept his voice quiet—they were out in the open, after all, and he wanted to keep his words for her ears only. "In fact, I do believe you were begging me for more. Stands to reason you might want to revisit things at some point."

Her face reddened and it wasn't from the scorching Florida sun. No, he was certain that she remembered that night just as well as he did, how they had burned for each other until they'd practically combusted. Heat like that didn't just disappear.

She was the one looking away now, first toward the still-closed door into the house behind them and then out to the lawn where flowers and ferns clustered in the shade of a sheltering oak. When she finally turned back to him she'd schooled her features, only the brightness of her eyes giving away the intensity of her emotions. The ice queen was back.

"I don't think there is anything to be gained by rehashing the past. But trust me, I'm not going to be begging you for anything."

"If you say so." He finished the last swallow of coffee and set down the mug. Now wasn't the time to push her. Honestly, he was surprised she'd agreed so quickly. He'd expected way more of a fight. "So how do you want to do this? Make a big announcement? Talk to a priest?" He was pretty sure she'd mentioned that, like him, she'd been raised Catholic, although neither was very active in the faith.

She shook her head, some of her hair escaping the confines of her bun. "No priest. This whole thing is bad enough, I can't handle lying to a priest on top of it." She gave a half smile. "That probably seems silly."

"Not silly."

"Okay then. Let's just keep things simple and quiet. The less fuss made the better."

He liked the sound of that. "We could always elope. Go out of town for the weekend and come back married. People do it every day."

She nodded thoughtfully. "I think that's the way to go. And once the news gets out about the pregnancy, no one is going to question it. We'll just say that we were dating back at the academy, and you followed me here to Paradise because you were in love with me. I was swept away by the gesture, and we ran off to get married."

It wasn't the truth, but it was believable. And it would get her under his roof and in his life. More importantly, the baby would be in his life. At least for a while. And if he planned to use the next twelve months to try and convince her to make their marriage a more permanent arrangement, well that was his business.

Because the more he was around Jessica, the more he wanted to be with her. He could only hope that she grew to feel the same way, or the next year—living with her but not touching her—was going to be torture.

Chapter Seven

The flu outbreak had ended as quickly as it had begun, which meant the station was fully staffed again, and Jessica and Ryan were able to be paired up with more senior officers. And good thing, because aside from the regulations about romantic partners working together, the chemistry between them demanded she keep her distance. But if just walking by him in the squad room was enough to send sparks flying how was she going to handle being married to him?

Even if their relationship was only on paper they would still be sharing a house. Seeing each other every morning and every evening, sharing meals—sharing a bathroom! Her face heated at the thought of being in such close proximity.

If this had a chance at working she needed to get a grip. There was no other reason her heart should beat extra quick every time she smelled his aftershave. Or for her palms to sweat when she found him staring at her across a busy room. She'd been attracted to him from the beginning, but carrying his child seemed to strengthen the feeling. She'd have to ask some of her mom friends if they'd experienced anything similar when they were pregnant.

Of course, they'd all been in relationships, if not marriages, with the fathers of their children. And she couldn't have asked anyway because she and Ryan weren't telling anyone about the pregnancy until later today, after they exchanged their temporary vows. As much as she was dreading the whole thing, she would be glad to get it over with. Ryan had made arrangements with a friend of a friend who was a notary to perform the ceremony at his office, on his lunch break.

Now, only four days after his bizarre proposal, she was standing outside a rundown strip mall staring at the window of a payday loan place, waiting for her soon-to-be husband.

She'd spent every minute since saying yes worrying that she was making the wrong decision.

Was she wrong not to tell Ryan about her inheritance? But then again why should she tell him? She had no plans to stay married. And it wasn't like she wanted the money for selfish reasons—it was going to help ensure she had enough to take care of the baby. Right or wrong, she had to do what was best for her child.

She glanced down at her floral maxi skirt and bright red blouse and found herself wishing she had something more appropriate to wear for a wedding. Which was silly, since it wasn't a real wedding. Still, she'd spent more time than she wanted to admit searching through her closet for an outfit. Unfortunately, even as early as she was in the pregnancy, several of her favorites had been too tight, especially in the bust. It seemed Mother Nature wanted to make absolutely sure she would be prepared to feed the baby, leaving her quite top-heavy at the moment. Her red blouse was her loosest one and the only one that hadn't showed an inappropriate amount of cleavage. She'd chosen the skirt because it was the only item she had with an elastic waist.

Oh well. At least they wouldn't be having photos taken so it really didn't matter. Still she felt frumpy and was tugging on her blouse when Ryan walked up.

He of course, looked perfect.

But then, he always did even when, as today, he opted for casual, in khaki slacks and an untucked button-down shirt. He should have blended in with the workaday crowd that populated the streets of Paradise's quaint downtown, but Ryan always managed to stand out. It didn't matter what he wore, he had a presence about him, a sheer masculinity that drew the attention of everyone around. Even now, as he reached for her hand in greeting, she noted several women checking him out.

Ignoring them, she let Ryan draw her toward the glassed front door.

"So, we are really going to do this?" she asked, not sure if she wanted him to reassure her they were or to call the whole thing off.

"We are. Unless you have a better plan?" He sounded chipper, which was ridiculously annoying.

"Unfortunately, no," she answered, her nerves—or morning sickness, or both—making her stomach roll like a ship tossed at sea.

He stopped, one hand on the door. "Are you all right? If you really don't want to do this, tell me now. I'm not trying to force you into anything. But I thought we had decided—"

"We did. And trust me, you couldn't force me into something if you wanted to." Like it or not, she'd agreed to this ridiculous plan, and she was going to go through with it. Straightening her shoulders she stepped past him and pulled open the door herself. "Come on, let's get this over with."

Ryan let out a breath, relieved Jessica had actually shown up. He'd laid the odds at fifty-fifty she just wouldn't show. He still wasn't sure how he'd managed to convince her. What he was sure of was that he was one lucky bastard. In a few short minutes Jessica Santiago was going to be his wife. Sure, it wasn't a conventional marriage, not yet. But he had a full year to convince her to make it real. Today was just the first step.

And really, there were worse ways to spend a day off than marrying a woman who was smart, gutsy, drop dead gorgeous and carrying his child. He'd never seen her in a skirt before, and decided the feminine look suited her just as much as her uniform, two sides of her multifaceted personality. It tickled him that she'd worn red—a color just as fiery as her temperament. Once again, memories of their night together filled his mind and stirred his body. He'd had a hard time thinking of anything else the last few days. Her "no sex" declaration had lit a fire in him. Definitely a case of wanting something more after being told you can't have it.

But then, it had always been that way with Jessica. She'd had an off-limits sign practically painted on her forehead at the academy. It had only heightened his interest in her then, and it had the same effect now. Of course, wanting and having were two different things. Good thing he didn't mind cold showers.

If Jessica was feeling the same tug of attraction she sure wasn't showing it. She had her mask back in place, the one that hid whatever was going on inside her, as she scanned the room. Probably looking for Greg, the guy who'd agreed to officiate in exchange for Ryan's help painting his house next month. Before Ryan could point him out to Jessica, Greg had stepped around the counter and was offering her his hand to shake.

"Hi, you must be Jessica. Congratulations."

She managed a smile while mumbling something that sounded like thank you, but Ryan could tell she'd been thrown by the well wishes. Stepping up beside her he gave Greg a one-armed man hug and tried to divert his attention away from Jessica for a moment. "Hey buddy! Thanks for doing this for us."

Greg nodded while motioning for them to follow him down a short hallway. "No problem. I figure I'm getting the better end of the deal. You have no idea what painters cost." He brought them into a small room with a round table and chairs, an ancient coffee pot and a set of dented lockers. "Let me just get my stuff and we'll take care of this. Do you guys have vows written out?"

Jessica swiveled, a hint of panic shining through her otherwise calm facade. Yeah, he hadn't thought about that either.

"With everything going on we haven't really had a chance to discuss that. Don't you have some kind of standard ceremony you can use?" He sure as hell hoped so. He'd barely gotten Jessica to agree to this plan in the first place. Any additional complications and she'd be out the door before they could say "I do."

Greg nodded as he pulled a small black book and a notary stamp out of the locker. "Of course. I just wanted to make sure. Some people get a kick out of coming up with something unique. But there's nothing wrong with sticking to tradition, am I right?"

"Sure." Because there was nothing more traditional than getting married at a check-cashing place. In his peripheral vision he caught Jessica rolling her eyes. Obviously he wasn't the only one to pick up on the irony. At least she now looked amused instead of panicked. That was an improvement.

"And you have the license?"

"Yup, got it this morning." Ryan passed over the document he had picked up at the courthouse on his way over. He'd been able to apply for it on-line, yet one more surprise in a week of surprises. Technology for the win.

Greg scanned it and set it on the table with his notary supplies. "Then I think all that's left are the rings."

Jessica shook her head. "We aren't doing rings."

"Actually, I thought we might." He pulled a small bag from his pocket, the local jeweler's name emblazoned on the front. "Just to make things look more official."

Greg raised an eyebrow, but didn't ask any questions. Not that Ryan really cared what Greg thought about their unusual nuptials. It was Jessica's opinion that mattered. He waited, and when she shrugged in acquiescence he let out a breath he hadn't realized he'd been holding. Logically, it was silly to care if she wore his ring. It wasn't like the small circle of silver would make the marriage any more real. But not everything was about logic.

"Well then, let's get you two lovebirds hitched."

Ryan reached for Jessica's hand and gave it a squeeze, and prepared to take one of the biggest steps of his life. Hopefully he wasn't heading in the wrong direction.

The only thing keeping Jessica from a complete panic attack was the absurdity of the situation. She was getting married in the employee break room of a check-cashing business. Who did that? The entire thing was ridiculous, and she was afraid that she might burst into giggles at any moment. Not that laughing could do any more to make the situation less dignified. Pretty sure they had already reached rock bottom in that regard.

Laughter was better than tears though. She had promised herself she wasn't going to cry. She would hold it together. No crying. No laughing. She could do this.

"Dearly beloved, we are gathered here…" Greg started to read and Jessica felt a giggle start to bubble up. Gathered? The room was empty other than the three of them. Ryan must have thought the same thing because he interrupted the pseudo ceremony to question it.

"Don't we need more people? Witnesses? I think the certificate has places for them to sign."

Greg's eyes widened. "Oh yeah! I forgot. It's been a while since I've done this, and usually there are at least a few other people. I've never had just the couple for a wedding before."

Jessica nerves latched onto the oversight like a drowning man to a life preserver. "Well, if we don't have any witnesses I guess we can't do it." She'd have to figure out another way to get her inheritance, or do without it, but she was more than willing to take this as a sign from the universe to call the whole thing off.

Greg shook his head, his grin annoyingly chipper. "Oh, no worries. I've got this covered." He crossed to the wall and picked up the phone hanging there. "Hey, Darlene. Can you and Lila come to the break room for a minute? Thanks."

So much for the universe offering her an out. A moment later two women in their early twenties walked in, both in the same blue polo and khaki pants as Greg. One was tall and thin with bleached blond hair and enough makeup to paint the Sistine Chapel. That one was Lila, according to her name tag. Darlene was a short brunette with the most impressive resting bitch face Jessica had ever seen. She was the one to speak first. "What do you want, Greg? If you're going to whine about people leaving dishes in the sink again, don't bother. It wasn't me."

"Me either." Lila tossed her platinum hair over her shoulder. "I'm on a diet. I didn't even bring food today."

Jessica couldn't imagine why she'd need to diet since there wasn't a single extraneous ounce on the woman, but kept her opinion to herself. She hadn't come here to critique anyone's nutritional habits. No, she was here to get married. Which really didn't make any more sense than the other, but it was what it was. A means to an end. A way to ensure some stability, however temporary, for her baby and herself.

"Nah, nothing like that. I just need you to witness a wedding."

Lila squealed. "You want us to be in your wedding?" She looked expectantly back and forth between Ryan and Jessica.

Jessica refrained from rolling her eyes. Barely.

"Not exactly." Greg held up the marriage certificate. "Just need you to sign this when we're done."

"Oh." A more subdued Lila shrugged her shoulders. "Okay. As long as I don't have to clock out. I can't afford to lose any hours."

"Do we get paid? Like actors or something?" Darlene interrupted.

"No, you don't get paid. And yes, you can stay on the clock." Greg shook his head in disgust. "Geez, you guys aren't very romantic."

It was the utter sincerity in Greg's voice that did it. Complaining that the *witnesses* weren't romantic, as if the rest of this situation wasn't an utter and complete dumpster fire.

The laughter Jessica had been holding back broke through. The more she tried to stop the harder she laughed until she was bent over at the waist, hands on her legs, wheezing in hysterics. Ryan's confounded expression just made her laugh harder, until tears streamed from her eyes and she could hardly catch her breath. She'd always had a tendency toward nervous laughter, often getting in trouble for giggling during church or while she was being scolded in school. But none of the people in the room with her knew that and they were all staring at her as if she had lost her mind. Maybe she had. Not that she cared what they thought— she was never going to see any of them again. Well, except for the one about to become her husband. *That* thought was enough to sober her a bit. Out of breath but somewhat under control, she straightened.

"You done now?" Ryan's somber tone almost set her into another round of giggles.

"Uh-huh. Sorry. But this whole thing is just so…" She struggled for a word to encompass the sullen witnesses, the low-end retail location and total lack of normality and shrugged.

"Unconventional?" Ryan offered.

"Weird," she responded.

"Very weird," he agreed, a bit of mirth lifting the corners of his mouth.

"Definitely."

"But we're going to do it anyway, right?" The uncertainty in his voice touched her. He was scared she'd leave, and knowing that made her feel a little better about staying. One more contradiction in the mess that had become her life. But hey, at least she didn't have to face all of this alone.

She could handle it on her own. She absolutely could. But maybe she didn't have to.

"Yeah. We are." Maybe this was a mistake, but it was one she was going to see through. "Just tell me what to do."

The ceremony itself was short, a blur of *will you* and *do you* and talk of a forever that she knew had nothing to do with them or their sham of a relationship. For better or worse might apply, but that was about it. Too soon it was over, Greg and their last-minute witnesses staring at them expectantly.

"Is there something else?" She'd tried to follow along, to make the right responses, but it seemed she'd missed something.

Greg raised an eyebrow. "This is the part where you kiss."

"Oh." A gaggle of hyperactive butterflies danced in her belly at the thought, which was silly. It was just a kiss. People kissed all the time without it being a big deal.

Of course, those people weren't kissing Ryan O'Sullivan.

Personal experience said that kissing him was a very big deal.

That was her last coherent thought before his lips were on hers, and her brain short circuited.

Heat surged from their fused mouths and filled her from the tip of her toes to the top of her head, lighting up every nerve ending in between. His tongue danced with hers, teasing and tasting his way past her defenses. One kiss, and she melted into him, her legs nearly losing their fight to gravity in the face of a much stronger force of attraction.

It was the sound of a door slamming that finally broke the spell.

Pulling back, she was startled to realize they were alone in the room. How long had they been kissing. And how on earth was she going to keep it from happening again?

Chapter Eight

As strange as the wedding had been, it was even stranger driving away by himself. They had taken separate cars there, so of course they left separately afterward. One more thing that made logical sense but felt completely wrong.

In fact, the only thing about any of this absurd, ridiculous wedding that felt right had been the kiss. It definitely ranked up in the top kisses of all time, beaten only by their first kiss back at the academy. Of course, it hadn't been just a kiss that time—or at least, not just one kiss. There had been a whole string of them, leading to quite a bit more, which was why were in the situation they were in.

Their first kiss as man and wife had been chaste in comparison, but had still stirred him enough to have him blasting the air-conditioner on high in an attempt to cool off his body and his libido. He'd kept his lips gentle, but she'd tasted as good as he'd remembered, the spark between them had grown into a full-fledged fire as the seconds ticked by. He'd noticed her legs weaken as she leaned into him and heard the stifled moan she'd breathed into his mouth. She might say that this marriage was just a business agreement, but that kiss said there was something more between them. Maybe it was just chemistry. Maybe it didn't mean anything beyond that. But if it did…well he figured he had a year to find out.

As he drove through the sparse weekday traffic he tried to tamp down the sense of urgency that rose every time he thought of their time running out. He needed to take this slow, and let things unfold naturally. No doubt Jessica was feeling overwhelmed by the pregnancy, and now she'd be dealing with letting her loved ones know about a marriage too, even if it was only a means to an end. She had enough stress on her plate. Pressuring her by moving too far too fast wouldn't be fair to her or to their unborn child. His job was to do everything he could to protect Jessica and the baby she carried. Even if that meant protecting her from himself.

He pulled into the driveway at Jessica's mom's house, blocking her little car with his own. She hadn't acted like it would be a big deal to tell her mom, but he knew she was dreading it. Of course, in true Jessica fashion, she couldn't admit to being scared or nervous. No doubt she would put on a brave front, just like she had when confronting a broken-bottle-wielding criminal. He'd had her back then, and he'd have it now.

He stepped out and met Jessica partway up the gravel path to the front door. He would have taken her hand, but she was already pushing past him and opening the door.

"Mama? Where are you?"

Mrs. Santiago appeared in the open doorway off the small living room, a partially folded bath towel in her hands. "I'm right here. Why?" She paused a few steps into the room, her gaze going from Jessica to Ryan and then back to her daughter. "I didn't realize you were bringing a guest over. I can go back to my room—"

"No, Mama. Stay. Ryan and I have something to tell you."

The older woman's face paled. "This isn't about your brother, is it? Did something happen on his shift today?" She twisted the towel in her hands, her knuckles white against the darker tan of her skin.

"No! This has nothing to do with Alex. I'm sure he's fine. You know he can take care of himself."

"Thank God." Sinking into a worn easy chair, she smoothed the towel across her lap. "I know you think it's silly, how much I worry about the two of you, but worrying is a mother's prerogative. Someday you'll understand." Jessica flinched at the comment, no doubt remembering that she would soon have firsthand knowledge of a mother's feelings and fears. Thankfully, her mother didn't seem to notice. She just smiled and waved at the couch. "But enough about my worries. Sit, both of you, and tell me whatever it is you came here to say."

Jessica seemed frozen in place. When she still stood silent after a minute, he stepped forward to stand shoulder to shoulder with her in solidarity. It wasn't his place to speak for her, but he didn't want her to feel she was in this alone. If he had his way, she wouldn't have to face anything alone ever again.

Jessica swallowed hard. She liked to pretend she wasn't afraid of anything, but all her bravado meant nothing when it came to her mom. She'd rather be hit by a Taser than see a look of disappointment in her mother's eyes. Dread coiled in the lowest part of her stomach like a viper waiting to strike. Taking a deep breath, she forced the words past the nausea and let them fill the room.

"I'm pregnant."

Her mother's jaw fell open, but before she could respond Jessica let the other bomb drop. "And married."

The old grandfather clock in the hall ticked off second after second of silence, her mother's rapid blinking the only sign that she hadn't actually died from shock, until Ryan stepped forward and bravely filled the void.

"I know this must be a surprise—"

Her mother cut him off with a rapid-fire retort in Spanish, the words flying so fast that Jessica could catch only a few phrases. None were polite.

"Mama!" Jessica tried to break in, but succeeded only in redirecting her mother's anger from Ryan toward herself. At least she was a more deserving target. She'd known her mother would be angry. But for some reason she'd expected the kind of cold, quiet anger her mother was known for. The kind that left you waiting for the other shoe to fall. The kind that had you begging for forgiveness without her saying a single harsh word. She'd been ready for that.

No part of her had been prepared for this hot

and fiery maternal rebuke. Without conscious thought she retreated a step, blown back as if her mother's tirade was a physical force. When the back of her knees hit the upholstered chair she folded down onto it, too drained and ashamed to stand against her mother's words.

Once again, it was Ryan who stepped into the breach. "Mrs. Santiago, I appreciate that you're unhappy, but you're upsetting Jessica, and that can't be good for the baby."

Was he right? God, this was hard, this second-guessing everything. But true or not, his words had the intended effect. Her mother blinked, and just like that the anger died down.

"A baby." She blinked again, her eyes filling. "My baby is having a baby." Her voice cracked, and a tear slipped down her face.

Jessica felt her own eyes misting. "Yes, Mama. I'm so sorry."

"Sorry? *Mija*, don't be sorry. A baby is a blessing."

Jessica shook her head. "Then why were you were just ripping into me in Spanish? I'm a bit rusty, but I'm pretty sure that wasn't some traditional Puerto Rican blessing. Unless selfish and stupid are considered compliments these days."

Her mom gave a watery laugh patting the cushion next to her for Ryan to sit. "I'm not angry about the baby. I'm angry that my only daughter ran off and got married without me! I'm the one who is stupid—not you—for not realizing my little girl was in love. I should have known."

Great, a whole new thing to feel guilty about. She'd known her mother would be upset to miss her chance at being the mother of the bride. Mother of the knocked-up newlywed just didn't have the same prestige. And now her mother was actually blaming herself for missing signs of her daughter's nonexistent love affair. It was too much to bear.

"No, Mama, we just…"

"Got caught up in the moment," Ryan supplied, keeping Jessica from blurting out the whole sordid story. "We're sorry we didn't tell you first, but it all happened so fast."

That, at least, was the truth. And it seemed to satisfy her mother. Of course, she was probably picturing a couple so madly in love they couldn't help but rush to the altar. Not a panicked mother-to-be hastily considering the pros and cons of housing and health insurance plans.

Or a woman desperate enough to marry for access to her money.

No. Her mother never needed to know that this was a marriage of convenience. Such a stupid term anyway—so far nothing about this was convenient. She would do what she had to in order to gain access to her inheritance, to make sure her baby got what he or she needed. But she wasn't proud of herself. And she wasn't going to break her mother's heart by telling her the truth. Lying might be a sin, but by this point she'd racked up enough of those that one more shouldn't matter. She wasn't trying to get to heaven, but maybe, if they managed to pull this off, she might avoid her own personal hell on earth.

Ryan examined the framed photos that covered almost every horizontal surface in the small living room. Most were of Jessica and her brother, Alex. But some were landscapes, tropical vistas of what he guessed was her mother's hometown in Puerto Rico. There were several of her mother taken against that lush green backdrop, both on her own and with other people he didn't recognize. Maybe Jessica's aunts and uncles, or old family friends. Only one showed the man that must be Jessica's father. An old, faded wedding picture showing two people looking very much in love. And very young. Younger than he and Jessica were now.

Was that why things between Jessica's parents hadn't worked out? Had they just been too immature, too naive to know what they were getting into? Wcre he and Jessica about to repeat their mistakes?

He watched her sitting with her mom, proudly showing off the ultrasound photo that the doctor at the hospital had given them, her face glowing despite the strain of the day. She might be young, hell they both were, but she was strong. And brave. And neither one of them was a quitter. They would make this work, whatever that meant.

"Well, I think I'll go grab a few things for tonight. I'll come back in a day or so to pack up the rest." Jessica's voice held a hint of uncertainty so he nodded in reassurance.

"That sounds like a plan. That will give me time to clear out space for your things." He watched her walk away and then shrugged, hoping he looked more relaxed than he felt. "Guess I should've thought of that before. Things just—"

"Happened so fast. So you said." His new mother-in-law raised an eyebrow and rose from her seat. "While Jessica gathers her things I'm going to make myself a drink. The occasion certainly calls for one, don't you think?"

"Um, sure, I guess. But I'm going to be driving, and Jessica…"

"Of course. Well then, how about some coffee? I had just made a fresh pot before you came."

"Coffee sounds good." He called down the hallway that Jessica had taken, "Jess, your mom wants to know if you'd like some coffee?"

"Tell her no, thank you. My stomach is a bit queasy again."

Her mother called from the kitchen, "Tell her I'll make her some ginger tea. That should help."

Feeling a bit silly to act as a middleman when they could obviously hear each other, he nonetheless repeated the offer, which Jessica accepted. He then found his way to the kitchen where Mrs. Santiago was screwing the lids on two travel mugs.

"I made the drinks to go. My Jessica packs lightly. It won't take her long and I'm sure you two are eager to be on your way." She pushed both across the counter to him, and then splashed a healthy dose of whiskey into her own steaming mug. "I hope you don't mind, but I'm not driving, I'm certainly not pregnant, and frankly I could use a stiff drink at this point. I'm very happy for you two, of course, but this has all been a bit of a shock. You can understand that, can't you?"

"Of course. And I am sorry—"

She waved off his words with a flick of her wrist. "No need for apologies. What's done is done. All I need to know now is that you are going to take good care of my little girl. Life hasn't always been easy for her, and I've made my share of mistakes raising her, but she deserves a good life. A good marriage."

"That's what I want for her too." He took a sip of dark sweet coffee, letting the caffeine work its magic. It had been a long day, and he and Jessica still had to work out how living together was going to work. He needed all the boost the drink could give him.

"Good, that's good. I know my Jessica can be difficult sometimes…"

"The best things in life always are." At least, he hoped that was true. Because none of this family stuff was looking like it was going to be easy.

"Are you two talking about me behind my back?"

"Just a little." He handed her the second mug, the one that smelled like pumpkin pie, the spicy scent filling the air.

"Nothing bad, *mija*." Her mother gestured to the tea. "Drink."

"Difficult isn't bad?" Jessica's eyes dared them to deny what had been said.

Unruffled, the older woman smiled over the rim of her mug. "No. Difficult is just difficult. But as your husband says, many good things are."

Husband. He was starting to like the sound of that. Which meant he was in for a world of trouble if he couldn't convince his new bride that their one-year marriage should have a longer expiration date. Like maybe forever.

Chapter Nine

Jessica leaned her head back against the passenger seat of Ryan's car and sighed, grateful he'd insisted on driving due to her nausea. "I am so glad that is over."

Ryan grinned as he backed the car out onto the quiet suburban street. "I bet. You warned me she wouldn't be happy, but I don't think I quite realized exactly how unhappy she'd be."

"That was nothing. Honestly, she took it better than I thought she would. She was more hurt than angry. And I think she toned it down a bit since you were there."

"Wow. Well, remind me to try to stay on your

mother's good side. If that was toned down I don't ever want to face the uncensored version."

Jessica laughed, the tension in her shoulders easing just a little. "No, you don't. Trust me."

"Now I know how you got to be so tough. The Santiago women are a force to be reckoned with."

"And don't you forget it! Now, if you don't want this Santiago turning on you I'm going to need to eat. Soon." As if to emphasize her point her stomach growled loud enough for both of them to hear.

Ryan winced. "Food. Hell, we never ate lunch. I'm sorry, Jess. I should have realized you needed to eat. Some husband—and dad—I'm turning out to be." He glanced over contritely. "What do you want? We could go out for a late lunch, to celebrate."

She shook her head. In a town the size of Paradise she was bound to run into someone she knew who'd want to chat, and the last thing she wanted to do was deal with explaining their situation to more people, especially on an empty stomach. She'd told her mom, and sometime soon she'd have to tell her brother, but everyone else could wait. "Could we just pick up some take-out instead? I'm not feeling very social."

"Of course. Burgers? Pizza? Mexican?"

Ugh. Ginger tea or not, none of that sounded

like it had a chance of staying down. "Maybe something…lighter."

She must have looked as green as she felt, because Ryan took one look at her face and changed lanes before turning into the parking lot of the local grocery store.

"How about I pick up what we need to make soup and toast?"

"That sounds perfect. Thank you." He really was sweet, when he wasn't being bossy and overprotective. A dangerous realization. Time to think about something else. Like balancing the need for food with her near constant nausea.

With that on her mind she followed him into the store and was immediately hit by the yeasty smell of baking bread. Her schizophrenic stomach rumbled again, flipping back into hunger mode. "Can we stop at the bakery? They make an amazing sourdough."

"Of course. We might as well stock up while we're here. Get whatever you like. I'm not picky."

Before they left the bakery section she had selected not only the sourdough, but a loaf of Cuban bread, a package of croissants and a box of guava pastries.

Ryan shook his head but wisely kept his mouth shut as he watched her make her selections. "You know what, why don't we split up. Take the cart and get whatever you want. I'll pick out a few cans of soup and come find you."

She shrugged. "Okay, but I'm only going to need a few more things."

"Sure, whatever," Ryan replied with obvious skepticism.

She did need only a few more things. However, it turned out the *baby* needed a lot more. At least that's how she explained it to herself as she tossed one item after another into the basket. When Ryan found her in the frozen food aisle she had a full cart and was holding a container of ice cream in each hand, trying to decide between them.

His eyes widened, but all he said was, "Get both."

"Are you sure?"

"Well, you *are* eating for two. So it seems only logical that you would need two cartons of ice cream." He reached into the refrigerated display and pulled out a third. "But this one is for me."

She glanced down at the label. "Plain vanilla? Really? Kind of boring, don't you think?"

"Classic, not boring."

Vanilla. She never would've guessed that would be his favorite—he seemed more the type to go for something more adventurous and exciting. Of course, Ryan was turning out to have lot of hidden surprises. He certainly wasn't the carefree, jet-setting playboy she had imagined him to be. At least, that wasn't all he was. Maybe in that context vanilla made sense. It fit with his down-home, working-class roots. Roots he hadn't actually strayed very far from. Would she be able to give their child that kind of a foundation? Or had her bad judgment ruined any chance at normalcy, for herself and the baby? She glanced at the cart and said a short prayer that the gallon of Rocky Road she'd selected wasn't going to be a metaphor for the path they were on.

"Well, this is it. Home sweet home."

Ryan's words cut through the worries that had preoccupied her during the ride to his house. Married or not, she couldn't think of it as *their* house. It was his, she was just going to be living in it for a while. She needed to remember that, and make sure not to get too comfortable.

Ryan must have mistaken her silence for disapproval. "I know it's not much…"

"No, it's fine. I mean, it seems great." She took in the small bungalow-style house, its stucco walls painted a warm saffron yellow. The yard wasn't big, but it was perfectly manicured. A row of gardenias separated the lot from the neighbors next door and offered a bit of privacy. It was a typical old-style Florida home and her heart was glad that this was the place her baby would first call home. "Seriously, it's perfect. Besides, you're talking to a woman who was living with her mother. This is certainly a step up. Unless you're going to nag me about eating my vegetables too."

He chuckled as he shut off the engine. "I might. Remember, I have a vested interest in keeping you healthy."

That's right—the baby. She needed to remember that the baby was the reason they were doing this. This wasn't about his feelings for her, but about his feelings for his child.

But knowing that didn't keep her heart from pounding when he stopped her at the front door and gently lifted her over the threshold. Taken by surprise, she clutched the front of his shirt.

"Sorry." His voice was low, echoing through her body where he still held her against him. "It just seemed the thing to do." She nodded and let go, smoothing the wrinkles she'd made in his shirt, feeling the hard muscles of his chest. Muscles that she had explored in depth. She'd been drunk, yes, but no amount of alcohol could have made her forget how good he'd felt.

In some ways that night seemed like it happened to a different person, in a different life. But risking a glance up at his face, their bodies still touching, the memories came rushing back. He was remembering too, she could tell by the way his brown eyes darkened to almost black, the way they had at the first sight of her naked body. Dangerous— that was how they looked, and this time she was going to heed their warning.

"Right. You just surprised me." As had the sudden rush of heat that had her whole body buzzing with…what? Lust? Attraction? Whatever it was, she needed to get control of herself. "Why don't you show me where to put my things."

"Of course. I'll give you the ten-cent tour and then grab the groceries. Maybe five cents—it's a pretty small house."

"Sounds good," she agreed, hefting the small overnight bag she'd refused to let him carry. She couldn't allow herself to become too dependent on him—it would just make things that much harder when she left.

"First, the living room," he said, stepping from the foyer to the right, into the front room of the house. Three square windows faced the street, with a low row of overstuffed bookshelves below them. She spotted a few recent bestsellers and their police academy textbooks, but most of the space was crowded with the largest collection of true crime books she'd ever seen. And there, under the far window… "Are those law school textbooks?"

Ryan shrugged, as if it was totally normal to

have half a dozen legal treatises lying around. "I find them interesting. And helpful to the job."

"A basic knowledge of the law comes in handy, yes. But these…" She squatted down and read the title of the thickest one. "*Advanced Constitutional and Civil Rights*, that's not exactly light reading." She looked again at the horde of crime novels. "In fact, I'd say anyone who has this kind of fascination with legal issues should go to law school."

"Now you sound like my stepfather." He rubbed a hand over his forehead as if trying to physically erase the thought. "Next you'll be telling me I'm wasting my intellect by settling for a career as a cop. As if police officers are somehow less intelligent than lawyers."

"Whoa, back it up a step. Do you really think you need to tell *me* that cops aren't dumb? I was commenting on your interests, not your abilities. I just figured if you were that into the legal stuff—"

"I'd be a good cop," he finished for her.

Not what she was going to say, but fine. It was obviously a touchy subject and she'd had enough drama for the day. No need to start a whole new round of it. Ryan obviously felt the same way, choosing to move back across the foyer and down the hall without waiting to see if she was following.

"The kitchen is where I spend most of my time,"

he said, stopping in the next room and letting her catch up.

"Let me guess, because that's where the food is?"

He grinned, the earlier tension gone. "You know it."

"I certainly do. I have an older brother, remember? Growing up, if he was home, he was either eating or sleeping. I'm not one hundred percent certain he didn't do both at the same time now and then."

They both laughed, and it felt comfortable. Like they really were a couple, making jokes and hanging out.

"Speaking of sleeping, let me show you where the bedrooms are." Ryan gestured for her to go first, and she continued down the hall to where it dead-ended in a door, with two more doors on either side of the hallway. "There's only one bathroom, I'm afraid. These old houses weren't built with a master bedroom either—both rooms are the same size and both open onto the bathroom."

"Jack and Jill—that's what they call a setup like that." Where she'd picked up that tidbit of knowledge she wasn't sure.

"Huh, didn't know that. Anyway, I've been using the room on the left." He opened the door and moved forward, leaving her no choice but to

step into the room. Not just any room, but his bedroom. With his big wrought iron bed right there,
just a few feet away. Part of her brain noted absently that he was tidy; there were no clothes
strewn around and the bed was neatly made up
with a lightweight blue quilt. The rest of her was
thinking about how good he'd look lying on it.
"Like I said, both rooms are pretty much the same,
but if you want this one—"

"I'm not kicking you out of your room. I'll take
the other one." The one just on the other side of
the bathroom, with just a flimsy pocket door for
privacy. She'd be steps away when he showered.
Not much more when they slept. Damn, but her
body liked that idea way too much.

Hoping he hadn't noticed her sudden flush, or
that she was starting to sweat despite the more-
than-adequate central air, she practically fled back
the way she had come. At the door across the hall
she fumbled with the doorknob into what was, for
the time being, her only private space.

"Is everything okay?"

"Um, yeah." Calling herself three kinds of a
fool, she finally succeeded in opening the door.
"I'm just tired. Would you mind if I lay down for
a bit before we eat?"

"Not at all. I'll just heat up the soup while you
rest. I'll let you know when it's ready."

"Thanks."

"And, Jessica?"

She turned back slowly, afraid he'd see her emotions on her face.

A decidedly wicked smile played on his lips. "Make sure you let me know if there's anything you need." He winked. "Anything at all."

Slam.

Ryan felt his grin widening. He'd been worried about Jessica, but anyone who could slam a door that hard couldn't be feeling too poorly. Maybe he shouldn't have provoked her, but he'd noticed the flash of heat in her eyes at the sight of his bed. He didn't have to be a mind reader to know what she was thinking—not when he was thinking the same damn thing.

Him. Her. Naked and tangled in the sheets.

So yeah, he'd poked at the idea a bit. He wanted her to know he felt it too, that heat that seemed to flash between them. Seeing her in his bedroom, he hadn't been able to resist. It was impossible not to think of how things had been, and how they could be.

And really, if they did follow up on the chemistry, what would be the harm? He pondered that as he brought in the bags from the car, and then dumped condensed soup and water into a pan.

They were already married. She was already pregnant. What purpose was served by denying themselves?

Backing off had seemed the noble thing to do, but that was before she'd gotten all hot and bothered just stepping into his bedroom. Before he'd realized that she was as hot for him as he was for her. Shouldn't they at least consider the idea?

He turned the burner down to low. The soup would keep, this conversation wouldn't. If she turned him down, fine. But he didn't think she would. She'd looked ready to combust, and he was more than willing to see just how hot things could get.

His body tightening in anticipation, he paused outside her door. It was still closed, so he knocked. No response. Another knock, and still no answer. This was foolish. Minutes ago she'd looked like she wanted to eat him with a spoon, now she was ignoring him? He'd done nothing to deserve the silent treatment, so why was she blowing him off?

Or maybe she was just in the bathroom, showering or something, and hadn't heard him knock. That made more sense. And was easy enough to check. Spinning around he ducked back into his bedroom and found the door to the bathroom still open, as he'd left it. Cutting through the small tiled space he knocked on the door connecting to her room, harder this time, and it slid partway open.

"Listen, Jessica, if this is going to work you can't just close me out…"

Except she hadn't. She wasn't ignoring him, or the moment they'd had. She was asleep. Passed out in the overstuffed chair he'd found at a yard sale. A book lay open in her lap; she must have dozed off while reading. Gently, careful not to wake her, he picked it up and set it on the nightstand, glancing at the cover. *A Guide to Pregnancy and Baby Care.*

He didn't realize she'd been researching. Was he supposed to be doing that too? Probably. Either way, the book and the look of exhaustion on Jessica's sleeping face were a one-two punch to his libido. He was supposed to be taking care of her, helping her. Instead he was letting the part of his body that had gotten them into this situation make his decisions for him.

Sure, maybe she was attracted to him. But she hadn't chosen to act on it. She'd chosen to walk away, to focus on their baby, not their chemistry. Pushing her boundaries when she was obviously overwhelmed would be beyond selfish.

Harnessing his hormones, he grabbed the softly faded quilt folded at the end of the bed, another yard sale find, and covered her as best he could without waking her. He'd let her sleep, and reheat the soup for her later. The shadowing circles under her eyes said she needed the rest more than the food.

Letting himself back out he retreated to the kitchen. He needed to rethink everything, and thinking was best done on a full stomach. Bypassing the soup and her fancy bread, he made a sandwich and grabbed a beer from the fridge. Definitely past time for a drink, even if there was no one to toast his mixed-up marriage with.

Mixed-up was probably too generous. How did you describe a relationship where you were married, but you and your spouse had never been on a single date? Not to mention the whole parenting thing. And all of this chaos currently had an expiration date on it—that was the part he couldn't handle.

Because no matter what they'd agreed to, he didn't want to be a part-time dad when this year was over—seeing his kid only on weekends, if he was lucky. Seeing Jessica only in passing. And she was young, smart and hot as hell. How long would it be before some other guy was stepping into his place, kissing his kid good-night before climbing into bed with the woman he wanted for himself?

The woman he loved.

Hell.

The beer turned sour in his mouth. He was in

love with his wife. Funny, he'd always assumed that would be a good thing. Of course, he'd assumed his wife would be in love with him too. Instead, the most he could say was that she was she was attracted to him. A good start, but a hell of a long way from love.

He pushed away from the table, dumping the uneaten sandwich in the trash and pouring the half-full can of beer down the sink. A beer buzz wasn't what he needed right now. What he needed was a plan. A plan to win over Jessica. He needed to figure out a way to woo his own wife, and he had a year to do it.

Chapter Ten

Pleasure. Her body was going to explode with pleasure. Every nerve ending tingled as she arched into his body, needing to get just that little bit more contact. Needing to feel herself come apart as he found just the right angle. "Please… Ryan…" And then even words were too much and she was flying. She reached blindly for the headboard, for his shoulders, for anything to hold on to as she rode that moment of pure bliss.

"Ouch!"

Her knuckles rapped against something hard and she opened her eyes. Where the hell was she?

Ryan was nowhere to be found, and she wasn't

in a bed. She was half lying, half falling out of the big soft chair in Ryan's guest room.

She'd been dreaming. That dream. Again.

Her head fell back against the soft cushion as her body struggled to separate fantasy from reality. She'd woken up like this, panting and flushed, half a dozen times in the last week. At least this time she'd climaxed…a few times she'd woken aching with need. That was way worse. If her sex life was going to be completely fictional it should at least be satisfying.

Gah. Thinking about it was going to get her all worked up again. Desperate for something else to focus on she took inventory of the room. She'd been too exhausted and well, horny, to take much notice before. The furnishings were simple. A twin bed with white sheets and a white bedspread. A simple pine nightstand and matching dresser. A small closet with louvered doors. Two windows, one over the bed and the other next to the chair she was sitting in, covered in a quilt she didn't remember getting. Had she somehow pulled it off the bed in her sleep, or had Ryan come in here and done it?

Oh, no. Had he come in when she'd been dreaming about him? Had she made, well, noises? Or worse, moaned his name? Her face heated again, this time with embarrassment.

"Hey, Jessica, you awake yet?"

Ryan's voice had her stumbling out of the chair, tripping over a foot that had fallen asleep while pinned under her. Cursing at the pins and needles sensation, she barely made it to the door without falling. "Yeah, um, just give me a minute. I'll be right there."

"Okay, no rush."

He sounded normal, not like he'd overheard her lusting after him in her sleep. So that was good. Besides, she couldn't stay hidden in the bedroom forever. Even if she could, she wasn't a coward. She'd face him, just like she faced down anything that stood in the way of her and her future. With strength and conviction.

And some serious bed head.

Well, maybe bad hair would keep him from looking at her like she was the last doughnut in the box. Because strength and conviction didn't feel like much of a defense against Ryan's Irish charm.

"Did you sleep well?" Ryan called from the stove, where he was ladling soup into a bowl. A plate with buttered toast was already waiting on the scarred wooden table, along with a napkin and spoon.

She shrugged. She'd certainly dreamed well. "Is this for me?" She waved at the set table.

"Yeah, I ate earlier. Sorry, I guess I could have waited—"

"Don't be ridiculous. I'm the one who flaked out and fell asleep." She crunched into the toast. "How long was I out, anyway?"

"About three hours."

She swallowed hard, nearly choking in surprise. Coughing, she reached for the glass of water he'd brought with the soup. "Oh wow, you should have woken me."

Ryan perched on the edge of the table, a dish-towel thrown over his shoulder. "Why? You obviously needed the sleep. I took the time to clear out some space in the bathroom for you, and finished up my laundry in case you needed the washer and dryer at some point. Or I'm more than happy to do yours with mine, next time I do a load."

She shook her head, her mouth full. The idea of their clothes tumbling together seemed way too intimate. And speaking of intimates…no way was he going to be folding her panties. Just the idea had her wanting to head back to the bedroom and hide. "I can handle it."

He shrugged, concern in his eyes. "Okay. But remember, the whole point of you moving in is to make things easier on you. I know I can't carry the baby for you, or have your morning sickness, but I can cook and clean well enough. Run errands, whatever you need. Accepting help doesn't mean you're weak."

Jessica blinked back a sudden rush of grateful tears. Her pride made it hard to depend on anyone, but he knew that and was trying to give her a way to save face. Even if she didn't take him up on it, she appreciated the sentiment. "Thanks," she said, meaning it. "I'll let you know."

"Make sure you do." To emphasize the point he grabbed her empty dishes, his eyes daring her to stop him.

She almost took the bait. But really, it wasn't worth arguing over, and if washing a few dishes made him feel like he was doing his part, who was she to stop him? "Thanks—for the food and the nap and cleaning up and everything. I'll make it up to you."

"It was canned soup and toast. You don't owe me anything. Like I said, the whole point of all of this was to make things better for you and the baby."

He kept saying that, but it still seemed like not enough of a reason to get married. She knew why she'd agreed to his terms—money. But what was *his* motive? Was it truly as innocent as he claimed, or did he want something more? She'd worry he was expecting certain…well…favors… but he'd clearly planned for her to have her own bedroom, and besides, that kind of manipulation didn't fit with the Ryan she knew. Hell, he had enough women interested in him, he didn't need to scheme to get one in his bed. So why was he doing it?

Well, there was one way to find out.

"And what about you, Ryan? What do you get out of all this?"

Ryan tightened his grip on the wet sponge in his hand. "I told you, I want to be a father to this baby, and I want to be there for you. I want to do the right thing." The truth, but not the whole truth. Only because she wasn't ready to hear all of it. If he told her that he hoped that their fake marriage would give them a chance to explore their very real feelings for each other she'd turn and run. And he couldn't risk losing her. So he kept his back to her, wiping down an already-clean counter, hoping she'd hear the sincerity of his words and not push for more honesty than their fragile relationship could handle.

She left the table and stood beside him, in his personal space, trying to rattle him. The more enlightened part of his brain was impressed with her interrogation skills. The rest of him was just trying not to notice how good she smelled.

She reached out and put her hand on his arm, stopping his ridiculous scrubbing of phantom dirt.

"Is that it? Is that the only reason you're doing this?"

He risked meeting her gaze, and the unease in her eyes broke something inside him. "I didn't invite you to move in so that I could have my way with you, if that's what you're asking."

"Of course not." She was trying for blasé, but he would have sworn there was both relief and regret in her voice. "I just know that there's been some…chemistry…and wanted to be sure that we were on the same page about that."

Hell, how was he supposed to handle this? If he said he wasn't interested in her that way, he'd be lying. But she needed to know she was safe here, or she wouldn't stay.

Taking a slow breath in and then letting it out even slower, he set the sponge down and dried his hands before taking both of hers. She jumped at his touch, and knowing he had that effect on her made him want to crow like a rooster. But he kept his voice measured, weighing each word before speaking. "Jessica, I asked you to marry me because I think that we make a good team, and because I think it's the best thing for our baby."

She nodded, and started to pull away. But he wasn't done yet. Still holding on to her, he continued, hoping his words would be the start of something, not the beginning of the end. "But I'll admit, that's not the only reason I want you here."

Her eyes widened, and he felt her tremble in anticipation.

"I'm trying to do the right thing, but I'm not being totally selfless here. Like you said, we've got chemistry. But more than that, I just plain like having you around. I like seeing you smile in your sleep. I like making you toast. Hell, I even like how you pick at things, like my interest in the law, or my issues with my family—that you aren't afraid to ask hard questions. And so yes, if I'm being honest I'd like a chance at more than just a pretend relationship. And maybe living together will give us that chance. But I'm not asking you to feel the same way, not now. I'm just asking you to be open to whatever might happen."

This time when she pulled away, he let her. But rather than step back, she stood her ground, her hands running through her hair in…what? Frustration? Confusion?

"Why do you have to make things so complicated?" She looked up at him, as if waiting for an actual answer to what sounded like a rhetorical question.

"Complicated how?" It seemed pretty simple to him.

"This was supposed to be a business arrangement. Now you're changing everything!" She spun away, and without thinking he reached out to turn her back.

He'd just wanted a chance to explain things to her face-to-face, but her momentum brought her crashing into him, her body instantly fitting against his as if they'd been carved from a single piece of driftwood. Carefully, he kept his touch on her arm light, letting her know that she could walk away if she wanted to, that he wasn't going to force her into anything—it had to be her choice.

Leaning in, he lowered his voice to a whisper. "Nothing has changed. I'll do what I said, and support you however you need. When the year is up, I'll respect whatever decision you make. I'm just saying that there's something to be said for going with the flow, seeing what happens…"

She shivered at his words, or maybe from his breath on her ear. He pressed closer, and she arched her neck, turning her face up to his instinctively. Longing filled her eyes before her lids fluttered shut and her lips softened. Accepting the invitation, he met her mouth with his, softly exploring, not wanting to overwhelm her.

He needn't have worried. Even as he gently nibbled at her bottom lip she was fisting her hands in his shirt, urging him on. Unwilling to be hurried, he kept his pace, thoroughly tasting her lips before finally delving in to the softness of her mouth. When his tongue touched hers she whimpered, a needy sound that tugged at his control. But still he held back, careful not to overpower her. Her body might be begging him for more, but he knew that once the lust faded she'd feel hurt and betrayed if she thought he'd used her physical reaction to manipulate the situation. And as good as she felt in his arms he wasn't going to give her any reasons to feel she couldn't trust him. He wanted this only if she did too—with her heart and soul, not just her body.

Jessica could feel Ryan holding back, and nearly growled in frustration. His patient, soothing kisses were all sorts of wonderful but nowhere near enough. Maybe it was the pregnancy hormones, maybe it was her body searching for a way to relieve some of the stress that had been suffocating her, but whatever the reason, his laid-back seduction was setting her on fire. Every inch of her skin craved his touch. Her breasts ached, her nipples hard with need where they pressed against the sculpted planes of his chest.

She knew he felt a matching desire, the evidence of his arousal was pressed against her, and yet still he kept his control, never crossing over into the type of passion she knew he could deliver—the type that would wipe her mind clean of anything but sensation. The kind she dreamed about every night.

Taking matters into her own hands, she grabbed hold of his shirt and pulled, freeing it from his jeans.

Working her hands underneath she ran her nails along his spine, grinning at the groan she elicited. Encouraged, she did it again, this time dipping down lower before working them around to his waist and then up his chest. She let her fingers tangle in the coarse hair she found there. Moving her mouth to his jaw she nipped and tasted her way to his ear. "Don't be careful with me." She didn't want his caution, not now.

He paused at her words, angling his head as if trying to read her face. She met his gaze, and whatever he saw must have met his approval. He gave a raw, feral smile before scooping her up and lifting her onto the counter. She wrapped her legs around him, gasping as he loosened the top button on her shirt and then kissed the exposed skin.

Yes. This was what she needed—to forget all the questions and the uncertainty and just feel.

She gripped the edge of the counter, focusing on the movement of his fingers, his lips. The pace was still too slow, but now she could feel that he was with her, no longer detached—his ragged breath tracking with her own.

He paused, his fingers hot on the swell of her breast above her bra. "Do you want to move to the bedroom?" He didn't say which, his or hers, and she didn't care. Both were way too far away. She didn't need a bed, she needed release. Now.

Panting, she shook her head and started in on the rest of the buttons herself. She'd freed the last one when the brash chorus of "Who Let the Dogs Out" echoed through the kitchen.

"What the heck?" Ryan's eyes darted around the room.

"It's my phone."

He looked like he might question the choice of ringtone, but then shook it off. "Ignore it."

"I can't. It's the ringtone for Cassie, my brother's wife. He was working today…"

She didn't continue but Ryan nodded, understanding. They both knew the risks cops took, and knew what an unexpected phone call might mean.

Pushing past him she darted to her purse where it hung on one of the kitchen chairs and dug out her phone. As she answered she said a silent prayer of protection for her brother. The guy annoyed the heck of her, but he was family.

"Hey, Cassie, what's up? Is Alex okay?" She hated that she always answered Cassie's calls that way, anxious and breathless. Cassie had become a good friend, but Jessica couldn't help but worry every time she heard that stupid ringtone. Her brother, knowing her fears, had been the one to program that song choice into her phone, thinking it appropriate for his veterinarian wife and probably hoping the silly song would make Jessica laugh instead of worry whenever she heard it. It hadn't worked.

"Alex is fine. But you're not!" Cassie yelled into the phone, the strawberry blonde's redheaded temper showing.

"I'm not?"

"No! You're pregnant! And married! And pregnant! *And you didn't tell us!*"

Oh, boy. She should have realized that this was going to happen. No doubt her mother had told her brother when she'd arranged for him to drive Jessica's car over. And of course he would have told his wife. And if Cassie knew, that meant she would have told their mutual friend...

"Hold on, Cassie, Jillian is beeping in." She swiped to switch calls. "Listen, Jillian, before you start yelling at me, yes, it's true, but it just happened and I was going to tell you—wait, are you crying?"

"Maybe, a little. I'm just so happy for you! You have to tell me all about it, every detail."

Jessica sighed. She'd known this was coming, but had idiotically hoped she'd get at least one full day of peace and quiet before the news spread. Obviously pregnancy was making her stupid.

"I can't right now—"

"Oh, right, I'm so sorry! This is your wedding night! I hope I didn't interrupt anything."

Jessica looked down at her gaping blouse. "Actually, Jillian, your timing is perfect. But Cassie's on the other line, wanting those same details." Tucking her phone between her shoulder and her ear, she fastened one button after another, her mind racing. She'd nearly had sex with Ryan. She had not planned on that. She had specifically planned NOT to do that. She knew there were reasons for the ban she'd put in place, but her befuddled brain couldn't quite remember them. She needed to think, and she wasn't going to be able to do that standing half-naked in Ryan's kitchen.

Or anywhere near Ryan, no matter what they were—or weren't—wearing.

"I'll come over—we can talk when I get there."

"Perfect! When?"

Jessica stole a look at Ryan, who was stalking toward her, his eyes still clouded with desire.

"How about right now?"

Chapter Eleven

As much trouble as her brother had caused her, while she'd been napping he and a fellow deputy had dropped her car off in Ryan's driveway and her keys in his mailbox without a confrontation. That would come later, when there were no witnesses, if she had to guess. But for now, she at least had a means of escape.

Ryan hadn't been happy about her running out in the middle of whatever was going on between them, but he hadn't tried to stop her. Jillian and Cassie, on the other hand, had been thrilled about an impromptu get-together, the latter quickly inviting herself when Jessica told her of the plan.

Jillian's house was nestled in the shade of a group of slash pines beside the historic Sandpiper Inn, a landmark on Paradise Isle. Jillian and Cassie were best friends going way back to when they were in high school and Jillian had worked part-time at Cassie's father's veterinary clinic. Now Cassie ran the clinic and Jillian ran the Sandpiper Inn with her husband. When Cassie had married Alex, Jessica's brother, she'd brought Jessica into her circle of friends. It had made moving to Paradise so much easier, and she was truly grateful for the camaraderie. Especially tonight. Maybe one of them could help her figure out how she was going to get out of the mess she'd made of her life.

She was almost to the front door when she heard footsteps behind her. Turning, she was engulfed in a giant hug.

"Oomph. Easy, Cassie, I'm breathing for two here."

"Sorry." Her sister-in-law didn't sound sorry in the slightest, though she did release her. "It was hug you or hit you. You got off easy."

"I'm reserving the right to hit her, for the record."

Jessica spun around, and this time she was the one doing the hugging. "Sam! I didn't know you were going to be here!"

The blonde gave her a hard squeeze. "Dani

called me, she can't come, one of the twins is sick, but I knew I had to be here. I figured it might take professional investigative skills to get all the details out of you." Sam was the only other female law enforcement officer on the island currently, although she worked for Fish and Wildlife rather than the sheriff's office.

"And how did Dani find out?" Jessica asked, hands on her hips. She wasn't surprised the busy lawyer hadn't been able to drop everything—aside from her legal career she'd also recently married a single father of twin girls and together they had adopted a son as well.

"Um…" Cassie fiddled with the strap of her purse. "Probably Mollie. I called her right after I called Jillian."

Mollie had worked at the veterinary clinic too, and was a mutual friend. She was also Dani's sister and another link in the Paradise Isles information highway. A long-distance link, given that she and her family were currently in Atlanta. No doubt whatever was discussed tonight would be shared with her later.

So much for privacy. If there was anyone on the island who hadn't heard the news by morning, Jessica would be shocked.

The front door opened and Jillian waved them in, the slight swelling of her belly betraying her own pregnancy. "I thought I heard you all. I wanted to catch you before you rang the doorbell and woke up Johnny. He fell right after dinner—pretty sure he's having another growth spurt."

"You look like you've had one too," Jessica pointed out. "When are you due again?"

"Not until November. I can't believe how much I'm showing already."

"Speaking of due dates," Sam asked, "Do you have one yet?"

"Guys, let her get inside first!" Jillian reprimanded. "But seriously, do you?"

Jessica rolled her eyes and made her way through the door and down toward the eat-in kitchen. The rest of the gang followed, and soon cartons of ice cream were being pulled from the freezer. Jessica thought of Ryan's plain vanilla as she scooped out a giant helping of Rocky Road. Was he eating it right now? Was he alone? She really should have stayed and talked with him about what happened. Of course, if she had stayed, talking wasn't what they would have ended up doing. Which was why she was here, surrounded by well-meaning but nosy friends.

Once everyone had been served and they were all seated around the big oak table, they started in on her. Sam, true to her word, went first.

"So, you didn't answer yet—when are you due?"

"I'm about eight weeks." She took another bite. "So due right before Christmas, according to the ER doctor."

"Oh, our babies are only going to be a few months apart!" Jillian squealed in delight. "But what's this about an ER doctor? When were you in the emergency room? Is the baby okay?"

Cassie answered before Jillian could respond. "Alex told me about the incident with the drunk guy the other day, but I hadn't put two and two together. That's when you found out?"

She nodded grimly. "Yeah. Some women take a home pregnancy test. Me, I faint on the job and get carted to the emergency room."

"Okay, so now we know about the baby," Sam said, taking control again. "But what about the father—I'm assuming it's this guy you just married? How long have you been dating, and why haven't we heard about him before now?"

"We aren't dating."

"No, you're married," Cassie helpfully pointed out.

Jessica shook her head. "No, I mean we never were dating." Three sets of incredulous eyes turned her way. "It was a one-night stand, all right? I'm not proud of it, but it happened. And yes, before anyone asks, we did use a condom."

Sam pushed away her empty bowl, and leaned in toward Jessica. "So, let me get this straight. You weren't dating, but you did get pregnant, and now you're married? To the guy you hadn't been involved with in the two months since he got you pregnant?"

"It's complicated." To say the least.

"I've got plenty of ice cream," Jillian retorted. "Keep talking."

Cassie nodded in agreement. "Go back to this one-night stand… How did that happen? When did it happen? How did you two even meet, anyway?"

"We were at the police academy together. After graduation we had some drinks and one thing led to another…and we slept together."

"Was the sex good?" Cassie asked, wiggling her eyebrows.

Jessica's cheeks heated as she remembered exactly how good it had been. But some details didn't need to be shared. "It was. But that's not the point."

"Hey, when you're married, good sex is important," Cassie argued.

"Yeah, about that." Sam pointed her spoon at Jessica. "Why *did* you get married? This isn't the dark ages. You don't have to marry a guy just because you get pregnant."

"She's right," Cassie agreed. "Trust me, I know all about unexpected pregnancies. They seem to be the only kind I have. Marrying Alex was the right thing to do, because we were in love. But I'm certainly glad I didn't marry Emma's father… That would never have worked out." Cassie's first child had been the product of a brief fling with a man who had turned out to be totally unwilling to be a father. Thankfully, he had given up his paternal rights so that Alex could adopt Emma. It had worked out for them, but Jessica's situation was nothing like her sister-in-law's.

"Like I said, it's complicated. We're not in love, like you and Alex. But he's a good guy, and he wants to be there for the baby and me. And the reality is, money is tight. Living together will let us save on rent and other expenses, and he'll be able to help with the baby care until he or she's old enough for daycare." By which point she'd have her inheritance, and the marriage would be over—but she decided to leave that part out.

"Hey, I've been a single mom, I get it." Sympathy shone in Cassie's blue eyes. "But this is a big step. You could have asked one of us for help, or your mom."

"No way. I mean, I'm not ruling out asking you

guys for babysitting now and then, but you're all busy with your own lives. And I'm not going to be a burden to my mom. She raised her kids—she deserves a break now. Besides, I'm an adult—I can't depend on Mommy to bail me out. I need to do this on my own."

"You mean with…" Jillian faltered. "What's his name, anyway?"

"Ryan. Ryan O'Sullivan."

"Still, you didn't need to get married just to live together," Sam pointed out. "There's such a thing as roommates you know."

She shrugged. "The family insurance plan is cheaper than each of us having our own separate plans too."

Cassie narrowed her eyes. "You don't really think we're going to believe you married a man for a cheaper health insurance premium. I know you better than that. There has to be something more you aren't telling us."

She sighed. She'd known they'd get the truth out of her. "Fine, there is, but nothing I say leaves this room, okay?"

"Can I tell Alex?" Cassie asked.

"No, especially not him. If he knows he might let something slip at work and then Ryan is bound to find out."

"Wait." Sam shook her head in confusion. "Are

you saying even Ryan, your new husband, doesn't know why you married him?"

"That's exactly what I'm saying."

After Jessica had left, Ryan had sat in his empty kitchen for all of ten minutes. Normally he enjoyed a quiet evening to himself, but right now, it was impossible for his mind to settle. He was too tangled up in knots over Jessica. She'd gone from scared and closed off to hot and heavy and then? He wasn't sure what mood she'd been in at the end. She hadn't stuck around long enough for him to find out.

Which, truth be told, really pissed him off.

He'd spent half an hour driving aimlessly along Paradise's nearly empty roadways, the spring smells of jasmine and sea salt blowing through the open windows. By the time he ended up at Pete's Crab Shack he'd gone from angry at Jessica to furious with himself. He wasn't sure if he'd blown things by letting them get so heated, or by letting her walk away. Or both. He just knew he'd screwed up, and now she was gone and he had no idea when or even if she'd be back.

And that sobering realization was why he was nursing a third beer at the bar, watching a highlight reel of golf, of all things. The first beer was out of anger. The second was for regret. And this one, this one was because he'd realized how pathetic he was, drinking alone on what was technically his wedding night.

Watching golf.

He took a long, hard swallow and considered ordering one more. Maybe if he got drunk enough he'd find the humor in the situation. Or better yet he might forget why he was drinking in the first place. He wasn't an experienced-enough drinker to really know how to predict this stuff.

He'd just waved down the bartender, a guy who looked old enough to have pulled beers for the founding fathers, when a hard hand on his shoulder spun him around on his barstool.

Dizzy from the motion and the booze, it took a minute to focus on the face staring down at him.

Oh, hell. And he'd thought the night couldn't get worse.

"What the hell do you think you're doing, O'Sullivan? Running off with my sister? Getting her knocked up?" A very angry Alex Santiago stood darkly over him, his fists clenched. He must have come straight from his shift—he was still in uniform. Which of course meant he was still armed. Not that the older man was likely to draw on him, but it sure put a certain spin on the situation. Behind him a few more of Paradise's finest formed an angry wall of blue uniforms.

Which was fine, he had plenty of anger of his own. Might as well spread it around. "What I'm doing is having a beer. Want one? I'm buying. Call it a wedding reception."

"I don't want your beer, I want an explanation."

"Well, you can have one after I get my drink." He waved his empty mug in the general direction of old Methuselah and was rewarded with a fresh draft. He took a sip, and sighed. "As for an explanation, it's pretty simple. Your sister is now my wife. And she's having our baby. As for how that happened, I don't think you want those details, do you?"

Alex reached for him, but one of the officers behind him managed to pull him back. "Hell, that's my baby sister you're talking about!"

"Yeah, well she's my wife. So we're even, okay?"

"He's got you there," one of the guys in the back said, laughing.

Some of the tension radiating off Alex eased, and he shook off the hand restraining him. "You really married her?"

Ryan picked up on the real question. "Yeah, I did. I'm trying to do the right thing."

Alex nodded in a reluctant acceptance. "Hell, man, in that case, I'm not sure if I should congratulate you or offer my condolences. She's not an easy woman."

Ryan chuckled and indicated the empty stools on either side of him. "Tell me about it. You'll notice it's my wedding night and the bride is nowhere to be found."

Laughter erupted all around him, and that was okay with him. Being laughed at was better than being pounded on. Turned out he'd been right, the fourth beer was the one that made it funny. Might have to figure out what magic the fifth one held.

Alex slid onto the next stool and at his wave the rest of the uniforms dissipated. Taking up his own mug, he took a sip.

"So, where is my sister, anyway? I was on the clock when Mom told me, or I'd have yelled at you both when I dropped Jessica's car off. And when I drove by after my shift, no one was home. You're here, but now I'm going to have to waste time hunting her down and starting all over again."

Ryan suppressed a smile. "Good luck, buddy. No offense, but my money's on her if you two go head to head."

That won him a rueful chuckle from the other man. "I'd like to say I win most of our arguments, but I'd be lying. She's got a stubborn streak a mile wide."

Ryan raised his glass in acknowledgment. "I'll

drink to that." He drained a good portion of the amber liquid before setting the mug down on the scarred wooden counter. "As for where she is, she said she was going to Jillian's house, whoever that is. She didn't really clarify."

"Jillian and her husband, Nic, own that big inn over by the beach. She, Jessica, my wife and a few others are all good friends."

"Actually, I think it was Cassie that called first." He strained his booze-addled brain to remember. "Yeah, Cassie called, and then Jillian, and then Jessica ran out, saying something about doing damage control. Seems news of our nuptials traveled fast."

Alex winced. "Afraid I'm guilty of contributing to that. But you gotta understand, I'd just found out that my baby sister was knocked up—"

Ryan raised an eyebrow.

"Excuse me, was pregnant by some guy I'd never heard of, and they were supposedly married. I was angry. Hell, I'm still angry."

"Understood." He'd beaten himself up plenty over the situation—he couldn't fault Jessica's brother for being upset about it.

"I didn't really think about whether Cassie would tell her friends. I just wanted to find out if I was the last to know or if Cassie was as in the dark as I was."

"No one knew, your mom was the first person we told."

"How'd that go over, anyway?"

Ryan drank deep to wash the taste of the memory away. "She wasn't thrilled."

"I'm guessing that's the understatement of the year." He turned toward Ryan, his face going serious. "You know, don't you, that it's not about the baby? I mean, she's a big church goer and all, and not exactly a fan of sex outside of marriage, but when Cassie got pregnant before we got married, she was fine with it. Said something about babies being blessings and started knitting blankets and booties. It's not being part of the wedding that she'd be angry about. And being kept out of the loop. She doesn't like secrets."

"She said as much, once she calmed down. Honestly, right now I'm more worried about how Jessica feels about all this than her family's feelings."

"Fair enough, man."

They both sipped in silence for a few minutes. When their glasses were empty Ryan gestured to the bartender for another round, but Alex shook his head and waved him off.

"Hey, what are you doing?" Ryan protested. "I'm only partway drunk, and I've got plans to get all the way drunk before I go home. In a cab," he added, not wanting his new brother-in-law, and fellow law enforcement officer, to think he was angling for a DUI.

Alex clapped him on the back. "New plans, brother. It's your wedding night, what'd you say we go find your missing bride?"

In the end, Jessica told them everything.

Jillian and Cassie both thought she should tell Ryan about her inheritance right away. "If he's as good a guy as he seems, he won't care," Jillian assured her. "After all, he still gets what he wants, which is to be involved with you and the baby."

"Unless you tell him, and then he wants part of the money," Sam argued. "If you're married when you inherit he may expect half of it to be his. If you divorce I mean."

"I'm planning on having the marriage annulled rather than divorcing," Jessica clarified. "But you're right. I have no idea how that would work, legally. Maybe he *would* be entitled to half of it." Her pulse quickened at the thought. She'd planned on spending most of it on a place for her and the baby to live and saving the rest for child-care expenses.

"You know who would know?" Cassie asked, clearing the ice cream bowls from the table. "Dani. She is a lawyer after all, and I know she's done family law stuff." She stacked the dishes in the dishwasher and returned to the table, Jillian behind her carrying a bottle of wine and a glass of iced tea. "Want me to call her?"

Jessica took the tea and shook her head. "No, it's late and she's got a sick kid. I'll track her down tomorrow."

"Even if you only get half, you'd still qualify for child support payments to help out," Cassie reminded her. "Or…you could just stay married. From what you are telling me he's half in love with you already…and you—"

"Had a momentary lapse of judgment."

"Which time? When you got pregnant, or tonight before I called you?" Cassie asked with a grin. "Seems like once is a mistake. But if you're still having a hard time resisting him, maybe there's a reason."

"There is—hormones. It's just all the hormones. Besides, even if I wanted things to work out, that's no guarantee they would. And I can't gamble my future on someone I barely know and have no reason to trust. No," she said, forcing a sense of confidence into her words. "Ryan's a good guy, but I can't be dependent on him. I need to know I can do this on my own."

"Still," Sam said, wineglass in hand, "why can't you at least get some action while this whole marriage scam lasts?"

"Because I don't want to blur the boundaries. Things are weird enough already—I don't want to confuse the situation."

They spent the next hour debating the ethics of Jessica staying silent about her inheritance, and had gone through a bottle and a half of wine and most of a pitcher of iced tea when the doorbell rang. Jillian sprinted for the door, nearly knocking over her chair in an attempt to reach the door before whoever it was rang again.

From her spot at the table they heard a loud, "Shh, the baby's sleeping" and then several sets of footsteps heading toward the kitchen.

"Who on earth could that be?" Sam wondered aloud.

Jessica's stomach tightened. It couldn't be Ryan, could it? No, of course not. He didn't even know who Jillian was—much less where she lived. And besides, why would he come after her?

Cassie stared past Jessica, mouth open, at whoever was coming down the hallway. "Alex, what are you doing here? I told my parents you'd pick up the kids after your shift."

"They called and told me the kids had fallen asleep watching a movie, and suggested we just let them spend the night. They'll bring them home after breakfast."

Cassie visibly relaxed, easing back into her seat.

"And as for what I'm doing here, this fellow seems to have misplaced his wife, and so as a fellow officer and brother of the bride, I offered to help him out."

"Ryan?" Jessica stood, nearly upending her chair as she spun around. "What on earth are you doing here?"

"I'm not one hundred percent sure, really." He shrugged, the loose motion a bit less coordinated than usual. "But your brother here seemed to think it was a good idea. And since he'd been nice enough not to pound on me, I figured the least I could do was go along."

Jessica turned back to Alex. "You were going to pound on him? For what? Marrying me? Or for having sex with me?" Alex winced, but she wasn't done yet. "That's right, tough guy, I said *sex*. I'm not a little girl anymore, and you, big brother, are going to have to get used to it. I can sleep with whoever I want to. And you have no say in it."

Ryan raised a wobbly hand. "Wait, do I get a say in that? As your husband I mean?"

At her perturbed look he backed down, but under his breath he muttered, "I'm pretty sure that was in the vows somewhere, is all I'm saying…"

"He has a point," Alex agreed with a smirk.

"You shut up. You had no right to interfere in any of this."

"He is your brother. Seems he had some right to know about his new niece. Or nephew. Or whatever," Ryan countered from where he was precariously leaning against the refrigerator.

"So you're on his side now?"

"No." Ryan shook his head. "I don't think so, anyway. I'm a little confused right now, to be honest."

"What you are is drunk," Jessica said. She tried not to sound judgmental. After all, the only reason she wasn't sporting a good wine buzz was her expectant state.

"Maybe just a little bit," Ryan agreed amiably. "But not as drunk as I would have been if Alex here hadn't showed up."

Jessica looked from one man to the other and sighed. "I don't even know what to do with that information."

"How about I make a pot of coffee," Jillian suggested, breaking in. "Seems like Ryan could use some."

"Irish coffee?" Ryan asked hopefully.

"Sorry, nope. I'm afraid we are all out of whiskey," Jillian replied, not sounding at all apologetic.

"That's okay. I'm fine with brandy. Or rum. Or—"

"Black. You're getting black coffee," Jessica interrupted.

"Man, not even cream and sugar?"

"Maybe," she conceded. "If you're good."

"Aren't I always?" His smile told her he hadn't forgotten what had happened between them earlier. The problem was, he was right. He *was* good. Amazing, actually. His kisses had made her forget her problems, forget everything. But she didn't have the luxury of forgetting. She had to focus on getting things in place before the baby came so that she could land on her feet if everything fell apart.

Ryan might want her now, but once he found out she'd married him for money, for access to her inheritance, that would be the end of any feelings he thought he had for her. Maybe she didn't know him well, but she did know that he valued honesty. More than that, he hated the way money had changed his family. To find out Jessica had done the same thing…well, it wasn't going to go over well.

Which was why he couldn't find out, not until she had a check in hand. She wasn't a mercenary— normally money was an afterthought for her, not a focus. But this wasn't about her anymore. Lying didn't feel good, but if that's what it took to make sure the baby inside her was provided for, she'd do it. She'd known about the pregnancy for only a few days, but already she knew she'd do anything to protect her child. Even if it felt like she was selling her soul to do it.

"You okay?" Sam asked quietly from the seat next to her.

Startled from her thoughts, Jessica glanced up. "Huh? Yeah, why?"

"Well, you seemed upset, unless you're going to tell me that napkin did something to deserve the torture you're putting it through."

Jessica looked down to where she'd shredded her napkin, the tiny pieces of paper covering her lap. "Oh."

"You know we've got your back, right? I mean, you'll have to ask one of the others about the parenting stuff—Dylan and I aren't quite ready for that yet— but I'm here for you. We just want you to be happy."

"Me too." Alex grabbed a barstool and turned it around, straddling it. "I know I give you a lot of crap, but it's just cause I want the best for you. If you tell me that this Ryan guy makes you happy, I'll support you. But if you want me to kick his ass…"

Jessica rolled her eyes. "No, I don't want you to do any such thing."

"So you're happy?"

She hesitated. Her feelings were all over the map. And the reason for that wasn't that Ryan was treating her badly—it was because *she* was keeping secrets from *him*. But she couldn't tell her brother that. So she simply said, "I am."

And if she was crossing her fingers under the table when she said it, well, no one needed to know.

Chapter Twelve

"You didn't have to drive me home," Ryan protested from the passenger seat of Jessica's car. "I could have called a cab."

"Don't be ridiculous. We're going to the same place. If you didn't want a ride you shouldn't have been out drinking."

That she was right annoyed him. Hell, now that the buzz was wearing off, he was feeling pretty annoyed in general. This was supposed to be his wedding night. He hadn't expected a picture-perfect honeymoon, but he'd been optimistic enough to hope they'd at least spend it in the general vicinity of each other. Maybe pop some popcorn and watch a movie. Instead, he'd been reduced to drinking. Alone. At least until Alex had come along.

"Your brother seems like an alright guy." From the stories she'd told, he'd expected a controlling jerk.

"That's because you're not his sister. He's over-protective and overbearing. At least, he was," she corrected. "He's actually gotten a lot better since getting together with Cassie. She's a good influence on him."

"Keeps him in line, you mean?" He'd seen the two of them interact. Alex might be a tough as nails police officer but it was pretty obvious his pretty wife had him wrapped around her little finger.

Jessica laughed. "Yeah, pretty much. He'd do anything for her and their girls. It's like he's a different person."

"Falling in love can do that to you." Ever since he'd realized he was falling for Jessica it was as if the entire planet had shifted on its axis, leaving him searching for his footing. It stood to reason the experience would be life changing for her brother too. The difference was that with Alex and Cassie it was mutual. With him and Jessica it was… Hell, he had no idea. Not after tonight. And he was pretty sure she didn't know either.

"Alex told me they got pregnant accidentally,

like we did. Seems to have worked out okay for them." He pushed, knowing it was a gamble. "Maybe it could for us too."

"Or maybe they just got lucky." There was an icy pain in her voice now.

"What you do mean?"

"I mean, for every Cassie, there's a single mom left on her own, trying to figure out how to stretch dollars and diapers until payday comes around. Having a kid with someone doesn't come with some guarantee of happily-ever-after."

"But it could for us," he argued, his native stubbornness refusing to back down. Yes, not all relationships lasted. But not all of them failed either.

"Or we could crash and burn. I can't take that risk." Her voice softened. "I know you want to pretend we're the perfect little couple, and when we're in public, I'll go along with it. But it's not real." She shrugged apologetically. "I know it sounds selfish, but I need to focus on me and the baby. Not a relationship."

Ouch.He'd just been relegated into the nonessential category, like he was a hobby she didn't have time for. And as much as he disagreed with her analysis of the situation, he also admired her willingness to sacrifice for her child. Even if it was at his expense. "That's not selfish," he admitted. "In a way, you're just being practical."

"Exactly."

Practical sucked.

With nothing else to say, he let his head rest against the cool glass of the car window, eyes closed. He was nearly asleep when the car swerved suddenly, and then stopped.

"Are we home already?" He blinked groggily. His buzz was nearly gone, exhaustion left in its wake.

"No, hold on, I'll be right back." She left him sitting in the still-running car as she vanished into the black night. What on earth was she doing? Was it the morning sickness again? He opened the door and got out, with thoughts of somehow offering help or at least consolation. They were parked on the shoulder of the road, near the beach. A thicket of sea grapes, their leaves the size of Frisbees, stretched in either direction along the shore. Rolling sand dunes lined the other side of the street. This part of the island was a designated wildlife area—there were no houses, no businesses, nothing. Just Jessica a few feet ahead of him, staring into the trees and, as far as he could see, feeling fine.

"Are you okay?" She must have seen something important to have stopped in the middle of nowhere.

"Yeah, I'm fine." She ducked down under a tree limb and inched away from him. "Just be quiet."

Fine. If she didn't want his help, so be it. He leaned against the side of the car, keeping one eye on her as he scanned the surrounding area. Nothing unusual. Maybe she *was* just feeling sick, and wanted some privacy.

A crashing sound in the bushes killed that idea. Running to where she'd entered the trees he instinctively reached for his weapon, remembering belatedly he'd left it locked in the safe at home. Alcohol and guns didn't mix. He settled for turning on the flashlight app on his cell phone, aiming the light in the direction he'd last seen her.

"Jessica, where are you?"

"Over here, in the trees."

As if that clarified things. There was at least a mile-long stretch of sea grapes along this part of the road. At least he could follow the crashing sound, which had a weirdly rhythmic cadence. "Are you okay?"

"I'm fine, but do you have anything to cut with? I need scissors or something."

What on earth was she doing? "Uh, no scissors but will a pocketknife do?"

"I think so."

She sounded close. He made sweeping arcs with

the light, and finally spotted her sitting down on the ground near a dense patch of underbrush.

"Oh, hell, Jessica. What on earth have you gotten us into now?"

Jessica bristled, even as she continued to soothe the big yellow dog she'd found tangled in the underbrush. Actually, they were both tangled. "I suppose I should have just ignored this poor creature when I saw it dart across the road?"

He sighed, rubbing a hand across his face. "No, I guess not. But how are you going to get it out of there? He looks pretty stuck."

"She is," she corrected. "She's a girl. And actually, we're both stuck." She shrugged, being careful not to move her head. "My hair got caught in the brambles when I was trying to get her out." Not her finest moment, but she didn't regret trying to help. She did regret that she had worn her hair down, instead of tucked into a ponytail.

"You're really stuck?" Ryan's lips started to curve. "You can't get out of there at all?"

"Not if I don't want to rip half my hair out. But if you toss me your knife I'll be fine. I just need to cut us free."

"How are you going to do that? You won't be able to see what you're doing."

"I'll manage," she insisted, sounding more confident than she felt. "Wait, what are you doing?"

"Coming to cut you free. And your buddy there." The dog wagged its tail in reply, the movement making a racket with each swipe. "She sure is loud."

"She can't help it, and I think it's amazing that she's in such good spirits. She certainly doesn't look like she's been very well cared for." The sweet golden retriever's fur was matted with burrs and mud and she was so thin her ribs were showing. Still, her eyes were soft and friendly and her tail had been thumping out a steady rhythm despite being hopelessly tangled in the Virginia creeper that grew in thick vines among the scrub brush.

"I wonder where she came from. I haven't seen any missing dog posters lately."

"Me either. She probably belonged to some tourists and got left behind. It happens now and then. Or someone decided to get rid of her and thought leaving her in a state park was more humane than taking her to the shelter. As if an animal that's been raised as a pet has any chance at fending for themselves in the wild."

Ryan bit off a curse, either at the idea of the dog being purposely abandoned or at the predicament he was in. He was halfway through the thicket, crawling on his belly like a navy SEAL. At least his hair wasn't long enough to be a hazard.

"Hang tight, Goldie," she assured the dog. "We'll get you out of here. Don't worry."

"You already named her, huh?"

Jessica smiled. "I guess I have. I didn't mean to."

He inched closer, his clothes covered in sand and dead leaves. "It fits her." He motioned for Jessica to duck her head. "Let me get you free first, then you can help me with her."

She angled her neck as much as she could to give him better access. His body leaned over her, their torsos nearly touching as he silently sawed away with the small blade he'd produced from his back pocket.

"There, you should be able to move now."

She gingerly moved a hand up to her head. "How much hair did you have to cut off?"

"Hair? I didn't cut your hair, I cut the vines."

"Oh, thank you!" She'd been afraid she was going to end up with a big bald patch on the top of her head.

He shook his head at her in amusement, and then worked his way further into the brambles to where the dog's tail was caught. "I'll cut her free if you'll talk to her and keep her calm."

Jessica nodded and lifted the poor creature's

head into her lap. "You sure got yourself into a pre-dicament, huh Goldie? Don't worry though, we'll get you out and make sure you are taken care of. You don't have to worry about a thing."

Wouldn't that be nice, not having to worry? Not about relationships, or housing costs, or medical insurance or which childbirth class to take? Heart heavy, she laid her face along the dog's soft fur and tried not to let her unease show. Maybe her own life was a wreck, but she could make things better for a dog. That she could do.

"There, she should be okay now, as long as she doesn't get stuck again." Ryan patted the dog's rump. "Maybe hold off on wagging that tail until we're out of here, okay?"

A happy thump thump thump was his answer. He laughed, the sound loud against the soft rush-ing of the waves. "Guess that would be too much to ask for. We'll have to figure something else out or you're going to get tangled all over again on the way out." He went silent for a moment, and then began to pull his T-shirt off.

"Um, what are you doing?"

He grinned, and continued to strip.

She knew she shouldn't stare, but damn. Ryan's chest was a work of art, a landscape of hard male muscle with a light dusting of dark hair. Only a few hours earlier she'd hand her hands on it and the memory had her blood heating. Impatient at the delay, the dog nudged her and whimpered. Nothing like a cold dog nose to break the mood.

"Keep her still, I'm almost done."

Forcing herself to look away from the distraction of Ryan's chest she saw he'd wrapped his shirt around the dog's tail, protecting the flowing fur from the thorns and branches they'd be crawling through to get back to the road.

"That should do it. The rest of her will be alright, it's the wagging that got the tail so tangled. If she wasn't so darned happy she wouldn't have gotten stuck at all."

"Don't listen to him, Goldie. It's good to be happy."

"As long as it doesn't get you tangled up in a problem you can't get out of," he agreed, starting back the way they'd come. This time he had no shirt to protect him as he belly crawled across the ground. He'd literally given the shirt off his back to help a stray dog. The gesture touched her in a way that his attempts to help her hadn't. She hated being the object of charity, but she could appreciate that same generosity when it was aimed at someone else.

She may have made some big mistakes, but she couldn't imagine a better guy to have made them with.

* * *

Ryan woke early the next morning, miraculously hangover free after a night of dreams about his wife. Ones that started with what had happened in his kitchen but, unlike yesterday, continued to his bedroom. Or his shower. Or on a blanket in the backyard underneath the stars. There had been several versions, all much more fun than the way the evening had actually ended, crawling through brambles rescuing a grateful but filthy dog.

Although even that hadn't been totally without it's rewards. He'd seen how Jessica's face had flushed when he removed his shirt. There'd been so much electricity hanging between them he was half surprised neither of them had gotten singed. After the way she'd walked out on him it was good to know she was still affected by him.

Too bad it couldn't have lasted. Instead, she'd purposely avoided looking at him and focused all her attention on the dog. She'd even, after assuring herself of his sobriety, had him drive her car so that she could sit in the back seat with Goldie.

When they got home she'd bathed the dog and fed it some hot dogs from the fridge before turning her attention back to him long enough to mumble a platonic good-night. Of course Goldie had gone into the bedroom with her, and now, as he peeked in through the partially open door, the dog was curled up against her new mistress's legs. Jessica had claimed last night that she had no intentions of keeping the homeless pup, but Ryan would bet his bottom dollar that the golden retriever was going to be a permanent addition to Jessica's household. She and Jessica had taken to each other instantly, love at first sight. He knew the feeling.

"You're a lucky dog, you know that?" he muttered, wondering how he'd ended up sleeping alone while this stray got to share a bed with his wife.

Goldie opened her eyes and cocked her head in confusion.

Ryan pointed a finger at her. "You heard me."

"Heard you say what?" Jessica asked groggily, squinting at him in the harsh morning light.

"Nothing." He certainly wasn't going to admit that he was jealous of a dog. "I didn't mean to wake you. I just wanted to see if you were up."

"It's okay. I need to call Cassie and see about bringing Goldie over there before my shift starts. Get her checked out, see if she has a microchip, that kind of thing."

He nodded. "I can call animal control and see if she's been reported missing."

"That would be great." She sat up, stretching her arms up over her head. The motion caused her ragged nightshirt to rise up, exposing a line of tanned skin above the waistband of her pajama pants that his fingers itched to touch. "You think someone is looking for her?"

"Huh?" He dragged his mind back from the erotic places it was trying to go, and attempted to focus on what she was saying.

"Just wondering if she has an owner, one that wants her back. You saw what bad shape she was in last night. She's cleaner now, but she's still way too thin. Either she's been on her own a long time, or she's been badly neglected." She stroked Goldie's now-clean fur, causing the dog to wiggle even closer. Lucky, lucky dog.

"Like I said, I can't remember seeing any fliers or notices fitting her description, can you?"

Jessica shook her head, sleep-tousled curls tumbling. "No. And I always check the lost-and-found board when I go by the clinic to see Cassie."

"So if no one is looking for her, there's a good chance she was she was abandoned on purpose." The idea of someone treating a living creature like a disposable object made his blood boil. "Well, as far as I'm concerned, she's welcome to stay here."

"Are you sure? You've already got me living here now, and then there's the baby coming…" Jessica bit her bottom lip, obviously torn between practicality and emotion.

Screw practicality. The dog made Jessica happy, and he was coming to realize there was very little he wouldn't do to achieve that. "Hey, every kid needs a dog, right?"

Jessica leaped from the bed and threw herself into his arms, wrapping him in an enthusiastic hug. For a brief moment he let himself appreciate her soft curves pressing against him, and then she was bouncing away, turning her affections toward the dog in question. Grinning at him, she ruffled Goldie's fur and dodged canine kisses. "Thank you, Ryan. I mean, maybe we'll find that there really was a mistake—that her owner is looking for her—but if we don't…thank you."

"Hey, I'm not your landlord, this is your home too. We're partners now."

"Still, thanks."

He shrugged, uncomfortable with how big a deal she was making of it. "No worries. Want some coffee?"

"Sure. I'll be out in a few minutes. Could you let Goldie out to potty while I get dressed?"

"Of course. Come on, girl. Wanna go outside?"

The big dog leaped off the bed and ran through the door, nearly bowling him over in her haste. "Hey, slow down. I'm the one with the opposable thumbs—you're going to need me to open the door."

His yard was fenced but he went out with her anyway, wanting to be sure she didn't dig anything up or find some secret escape route. If she stayed he'd make sure the fence was totally dog proof. It wouldn't do for her to get herself lost again.

For now, he straddled one of the two folding chairs he'd bought for the small concrete patio. Resting his arms on the back of the chair he watched the dog explore her new territory and found himself hoping she stayed. Jessica probably didn't realize it, but she seemed to relax her guard when she was around Goldie, dropping the protective wall he'd been banging his head against since the first day they met. Besides, taking care of the dog would give him and Jessica a chance to practice their teamwork before the baby came. And when it came to winning over his wife he was going to need all the help he could get.

If that help came with soft fur and a wagging tail, well that was just fine.

The Paradise Animal Clinic waiting room was a zoo of activity when Jessica walked in an hour later. An elderly man held an angry Chihuahua in his lap, the miniature menace doing his best to intimidate the bored Great Dane lying on the floor a few feet away. Two cats in matching pink cat carriers were meowing in protest at their current confinement, and a parakeet had gotten loose and was darting back and forth just out of reach of the tattooed and potbellied man trying to catch it. Goldie, apparently not used to such commotion, whimpered and huddled into Jessica's side.

She rubbed the nervous dog's soft ears soothingly. "It's okay, baby. It's a little overwhelming, but this is a safe place, I promise. They like doggies here."

"We sure do." Cassie said from an exam room doorway. "But where did you find this one?"

Jessica led Goldie over to her sister-in-law. "Running across the road, over by the beach. I nearly hit her."

"Oh no! She's lucky you didn't. We see a lot of canine versus car injuries, and the car always wins. I wonder where she came from."

"I was hoping you could help me with that. She wasn't wearing a collar or anything, but I thought you might recognize her."

Cassie cocked her head in thought as she looked the dog over. "No, I don't think so. But we'll scan her and see if she has a microchip. Most shelters implant them now, and a lot of breeders do too. Not everyone keeps up with the registration, but if she has one it will give us a place to start."

She turned and ducked her head back into the exam room, where a young boy was futilely trying to drag a dog twice his size toward the door. "Jimmy, your mom will be done paying the bill in a minute. Why don't you let her handle Bruno, okay?"

The boy tugged once more, his face straining as he leaned all his weight on the leash, before nodding in defeat. Cassie smiled and headed for the main treatment room, motioning for Jessica to follow her. Behind the scenes, things were even more chaotic than up-front. A row of gleaming metal cages held half a dozen resident patients, some with IV drips, some sleeping, and one feisty puppy who was digging furiously in his food bowl, scattering kibble everywhere.

"Busy day, huh?" Jessica asked, even as an employee in scrubs pushed a chart into Cassie's hands. Cassie looked down, made a notation, and handed it back before answering.

"Yup. But hey, at least it isn't boring. Dad's coming in this afternoon, so that'll help." Cassie's father was still a partner in the clinic, but he was semiretired now.

"I'm sorry to bother you. I could come back later." She probably should have called first.

"Nonsense." Cassie reached into a cabinet and removed an oblong plastic device. "It'll only take a few minutes to scan this pretty girl, and if we can reunite her with her owner it will be well worth the time." She ran the scanner over the dog's neck and shoulders, holding it up in triumph when it beeped. "Got it!"

Jessica's heart sank. She should be glad, but in her heart she'd already started to think of Goldie as hers. "Now what?"

"Now we call it in to a central clearinghouse." The young vet copied the string of numbers from the device's screen onto a pad of paper. "If we're lucky they'll match this number up with her owner's information. Or, if it's still registered to the shelter or breeder she came from we'll call them, and see if they can track down who she belongs to."

"I can do that." Jessica reached for the paper, fighting the urge to rip it up and pretend she'd never seen it.

"Okay, the number to call is here, on the back of the scanner." She handed it over along with the paper. "You can use the phone in my office. Let me know if you run into any trouble."

Office was a generous term for the closet-sized space that housed Cassie's desk, a computer and stacks of veterinary textbooks and medical journals. But it had a phone, and, with the door closed, offered a bit of quiet compared to the chaos outside.

After dialing the number, it took several minutes to navigate the automated menu, but finally she got a human being on the line. One who was more than happy to share all the information he had on Goldie. Except Goldie's real name was Chloe, and she belonged to a man named Clive Redmond.

Jessica numbly wrote down the owner's contact information and hung up. Goldie/Chloe rested her head in Jessica's lap, perhaps sensing something important was happening. Absently, Jessica stroked her silky fur and dialed.

"Hello?" a groggy voice answered on the third ring.

"Hi, I'm looking for Clive Redmond?"

"Well you found him. What do you want?"

She took a deep breath, and forced herself to sound polite. "I wanted to let you know I found your dog last night."

"Lady, I don't have a dog."

"A golden retriever, named Chloe?" she persisted. "The microchip company said she's registered to your name."

"Ah, hell. That dog? She ran away months ago. I only adopted her because my old lady wanted a dog, but she took off a week after I got the dang thing and left the stupid mutt with me. When it ran off too, I figured good riddance to both of them."

Goldie/Chloe whined, and Jessica realized she was clenching her hands in the dog's fur. Relaxing her fingers, Jessica forced herself to stay calm.

Yelling at this loser wasn't going to help anyone, even if he did have it coming. "So does that mean you don't want her back?"

"Hell no. I can't afford to feed myself, let alone some smelly dog. As far as I'm concerned, you can keep her." A sharp click ended the conversation.

Shocked, Jessica looked down at the soft, trusting eyes staring at her and wondered how anyone could be so hard-hearted. "So, what do we do now, Goldie?" No way was she going to use the name that horrid man had given the dog. A soft wag was the dog's only reply. "Is it wrong that I want to keep you? I'm pregnant, and I'm sort of freaking out about that. And I just started a new job that's going to keep me really busy. And on top of everything else I went and got married. So you see, my life is really complicated right now."

Goldie gave her arm a gentle nudge, sneaking her head further into Jessica's lap.

Giving in, Jessica dropped a kiss on the gentle dog's nose. "Welcome to the family."

Chapter Thirteen

Despite Jessica's worries, Goldie slid seamlessly into her life as if she'd always been there. In fact, there were days when Goldie's happy wag and loyal companionship were the only things keeping Jessica sane. She was still on the night shift, although no longer partnered up with Ryan. Thankfully her superiors at the department had taken news of her marriage and pregnancy in stride, simply advising her to keep them apprised of any medical issues that might affect her performance or safety, and asking that she fill out all the paperwork for her maternity leave well in advance. She'd be allowed to continue her regular duties until and unless she requested to be moved to a desk job. Figuring out how to order a maternity uniform had been the most difficult part.

Among her fellow deputies, however, the news had made a bigger stir. But it wasn't that she was pregnant that attracted the most attention—it was their sudden elopement that had really greased the gears of the gossip mill. Everyone wanted to know when they'd met, how long they'd been dating, why they'd kept their romance a secret. She'd floundered at first, leading several to speculate about a shotgun wedding, with the suggestion that her brother had held the proverbial gun.

Alex, thankfully, had denied those rumors and admitted he hadn't known about the wedding until after the fact. She didn't mind people thinking she'd gotten married because of the baby, it was true after all. But the idea that she'd been forced to marry, that her brother had made that decision for her as if she was some kind of pawn to be ordered around—that infuriated her. As did the insinuation that Ryan had only proposed under duress. Something she'd explained to Cassie one night with a few tears and way too much ice cream.

She suspected Cassie was behind Alex's quick and vocal reaction to that particular rumor. Her sister-in-law had been incredibly supportive. So had Ryan. There had been no more kissing in the kitchen, or anywhere else, but as her belly had grown so had their friendship. They often worked different hours, but no matter how tired he was or how many hours he'd been on his feet, Ryan somehow always made time to cook her a hot meal each day. She'd thrown up probably half of them in the first few months, but now, at the tail end of her second trimester, she was able to fully appreciate them. He'd even taken to sneaking snacks into her purse and water bottles into her car.

There'd been no more talk of a real relationship, no more pushing for more than she could give. Which, she reminded herself daily, was a good thing. Except just like a kid who'd been told not to touch the candy bowl, she found herself wanting what she couldn't—or shouldn't—have.

Who wouldn't like a guy that always made time to throw the tennis ball for the dog, replaced the toilet paper roll the right way and kept her favorite bubble bath in stock at all times?

And it wasn't like he was hard on the eyes. He'd started running with Goldie every morning, and spending extra time in the gym after his shift. And wow, did it show. He'd always been fit, but now he looked like he should be in one of those charity calendars with the half-naked men. Around town she couldn't go a day without someone telling her how lucky she was to have such a handsome husband. But lucky wasn't how she felt when she was lying alone in her bed, unable to stop thinking about him and the one night they'd spent together. If she gave in and let it happen again, would it be as good as she remembered? Or had her memories of their lovemaking been fueled more by tequila than reality?

Not that she was going to find out. They had a plan, a course of action, and that was just the way things had to be. Besides, even if she wanted to change things, it was too late. He'd muscled up, getting hotter by the day, but she'd ballooned out until she resembled a whale. A glance in the full length mirror on her bedroom door confirmed it—she was huge. And she still had another three more months to go!

No, she wasn't going to be seducing anyone, not in her condition. Which was for the best. Right now she and Ryan had a good working relationship, which was what they were going to need when the baby came. No point in rocking the boat. Besides, she felt too guilty about keeping the information about her inheritance from him to feel comfortable asking for more from their relationship. She didn't deserve his trust when she'd been lying by omission the whole time. Months of hiding something this big from him was eating a hole in her soul.

He'd trusted her with so much—his home, his family history, his last name. Meanwhile, she was keeping a secret of epic proportions. She'd been so worried he might use the information against her, or demand a share of the money, but the man she knew now would never be so petty. Her friends had been right, she should have told him about the inheritance right from the start. Now it was too late.

Maybe once she had the money in her hands it would seem worth it. She'd started the process to claim the inheritance, but it wasn't as simple as she'd hoped. There were hoops to jump through, but the law firm was supposed to be sending over the last of the paperwork any time now, and Dani had assured her that she'd help Jessica fill it out. Once the baby was born and she'd turned over a copy of the birth certificate, she'd be getting a very large check. She'd even started keeping an eye on the for sale section of a popular real estate website, logging in when Ryan wasn't around and feeling guilty every time she clicked on a link. Sooner or later he would find out, but later seemed a lot better than now.

A quick knock at the door pulled her from her thoughts. "Are you ready to go?"

"Coming!" She grabbed her duffle bag off the foot of the bed and opened the door to find Ryan waiting in the hall, a concerned look on his face.

"You don't have to play, you know. It's not required."

The annual red vs. blue softball game was today, the Paradise tradition pitting the sheriff's department against the fire department. She was playing third base, and Ryan was not happy about it.

"I know I don't have to play. I *want* to play." She'd been on the varsity team in high school— no way was she going to miss out on a chance to enjoy the game again.

"But the baby—"

"Will be fine." She put a protective hand over her bump. "The doctor said exercise is good for me and the baby." She'd kept up with her gym time as well, but at a much slower pace than Ryan. "There's no reason I can't join in, so you can stop trying to convince me."

"Fine." He jammed his ball cap further down in frustration. "But if you have any pain at all, or anything feels weird—"

"I'll bench myself. I promise." She hadn't made it this far to risk hurting her baby. Their baby. But she also wasn't going to let his overprotectiveness keep her from having a good time. The same went for Alex. He'd be at the game too, and would probably be just as upset with her playing as Ryan was. Heaven help her, they meant well but good intentions didn't mean they weren't going to drive her up the wall before she gave birth. Maybe that was why they said pregnant women were unreasonable. It wasn't the hormones, it was dealing with the men in their lives that made them that way.

Ryan was starting to think it would have been better if Jessica had been the one to drive to the ball field, because he was having a really hard time keeping his eyes on the road. It was hard enough to keep his lust for his wife under control when she was fully covered in baggy sweats or a boxy uniform, and today she'd was wearing a tight tank top that made no pretense of hiding her very feminine figure, the scoop-necked shirt revealing enough cleavage to have him ready to forget the game and turn right back around.

It wasn't just the outfit, though. She had an aura of sexuality about her, and it was only increasing as the pregnancy progressed. Maybe it was the glow of her skin, or the way her still-athletic appearance was balanced by the softer curves, or maybe it was just some kind of primitive pheromone reminding him that that was his baby inside her. All he knew was he was walking around in a near-constant state of arousal. He'd tried channeling his frustration into his workouts, but he could spend only so many hours in the gym and he'd worn out the poor dog with all the miles they'd run.

Cold showers helped, but what he really needed was Jessica in his bed all night long. Hell, at this point, a night might not be long enough. A long weekend maybe, with brief breaks for food and sleep.

Too bad she'd shown no signs of softening her business-only approach to their relationship. As it was, the only one allowed in her bed was Goldie, and that situation didn't seem likely to change. At least she was becoming more accepting of his presence in her life, no longer bristling when he offered to help her do something. They seemed to have worked out a pleasant but platonic partnership based on friendship and a mutual interest in their baby. But there was always an unspoken line that neither of them dared to cross.

He'd tried to be content with the progress of their relationship, telling himself that if he was patient the chemistry that still boiled beneath the surface would naturally lead to something more. But it had been months now, and the only thing he had to show for it was a faster mile and a personal record for the bench press. The need for things to move faster, further was building but he knew he couldn't push. If Jessica hated anything it was overbearing men trying to tell her what to do or how to feel. Forcing a conversation she wasn't ready for would just send her running. And as much as he wanted to make her his wife in every way, he wasn't willing to give up the ground he'd gained. He was in this for the long haul. Nothing short of everything would be enough.

In the meantime, they'd play ball.

The ball fields were part of a larger municipal park, and the place was packed. It seemed most of the town had come out to enjoy the early fall weather. Parents ringed the playground, talking with each other as they supervised herds of rambunctious children clambering over playground equipment, and joggers dotted the trails. Ryan and Jessica passed a heated game of pickup basketball and several seniors playing shuffleboard before arriving at the designated softball field. Beside him, enthusiasm pulsed off Jessica in waves. Still, the thought of her ending up in the path of a hard hit line drive made his palms sweat.

"You're sure about this?" he asked again as they made their way to the dugout.

"Heck, yeah I am." She removed a well-worn leather glove from her bag and pulled it on, punching her fist into it. "Fire and rescue doesn't stand a chance."

He laughed and shook his head. "They sure don't." And neither did he. Jessica was a force of nature, and it would take a far greater man than him to stand against her. Not that he wanted to. He

liked that they were really feeling like a team—
even now, when they were part of a bigger team
that was about to take the field.

Jessica trotted off to third base, her tank top
now covered by a baggy team T-shirt. The view
was better before, but maybe now he'd be able to
keep his mind on the game. Taking his own place
at second he tried to focus. The first batter struck
out, triggering both cheers and good natured trash
talk from the opposing factions in the stands. The
second tipped up a high flying foul that the catcher
had no trouble turning into a second out.

The third player in the line up stepped up to the
plate. A mountain of a man, Jimmy Akers dwarfed
the other players. Holding a bat that looked way
too small next to his sizable bulk, he nodded con-
fidently at the pitcher as if daring him to throw a
strike.

Out of the corner of his eye Ryan noticed Jessica crouch in readiness. The other fielders shuf-
fled in unease—wherever this ball went it was
going to go there hard and fast.

"Strike one!" the umpire called, after a pitch
flew by with no reaction from Jimmy.

The next pitch was a repeat of the first.

Ryan started to relax. The guy was big, but
that didn't mean he was a good hitter. Hitting

took hand-eye coordination, not brute strength. Maybe he'd get shut down without so much as a swing.

Crack!

Or maybe he had just been waiting for his perfect pitch. Like a rocket the ball shot down the inside of the third base foul line, and Jessica was there waiting for it. His breath caught…a straight drive like that could knock a player senseless. If she got hit—

But no. She snatched the ball out of midair without so much as a flinch, closing this half of the inning with a third out. Damn, that woman was tough. Jumping in delight she flashed him a triumphant smile as he headed her way. "That was a helluva catch!"

She smirked. "Not bad for a pregnant lady, huh?"

"Not bad, period." He followed her into the dugout where she was greeted with high fives by several players.

She shrugged off the attention and stowed her glove under the bench. "I told you I could play."

"Yes, you did. You just didn't say how well. Are you as good at batting at you are at fielding?"

She winked, her cheeks flushed with excitement. "You'll just have to wait and see, won't you?"

* * *

Jessica's breath came fast as she ran hard to first base, stopping at the coach's hand signal. A single was respectable, especially given how quickly a few of her teammates had struck out. But the exhilaration of running the bases wasn't the only reason for her pounding pulse. No, what had her heart beating out of her chest was the man walking up to the on deck circle, looking like God's gift to sports. He shouldn't have been so sexy wearing old sweats and the same team shirt as everyone else, and yet, he was. He *so* was.

Even as she forced herself to watch the current batter, her body remained aware of Ryan's every move. She couldn't help but notice the confidence in his stance as he stretched, or the way his eyes had been following her all day. At first he'd looked nervous, but after she'd snatched that line drive in the first inning he'd seemed more proud than concerned. Unlike her brother and mother, who between them had asked her no less than twice per inning if she felt okay or if she needed to rest. No, Ryan managed to care without being overbearing. After a lifetime of feeling nearly smothered to death by her family's well-meaning concern it was refreshing to have her abilities respected.

The player at the plate struck out, and Ryan took his place in the batter's box. He caught her staring and a cocky grin broke over his face. Darn him and his ego! She was a base runner, she was *supposed* to be watching the batter—it didn't mean anything that she had her eyes on him. But of course none of the other players made her face heat and her skin tingle. *Focus, Jessica, focus*.

The pitcher sent a fastball over the plate. Ryan, moving as if he had all the time in the world, eyed the pitch and swung, the bat connecting with a satisfying thud.

Jessica took off, her feet pounding the red clay as she headed for second.

"Go, go!" the third base coached yelled over the din of the crowd, his arm windmilling as he waved her on to third. Nodding, she pumped her arms harder and kept going, barely touching the base before heading for home.

Her shoe smacked against the plate but momentum carried her several yards farther. Yes! A quick celebratory fist pump and then Ryan was heading her way. Running hard, his eyes met hers, and suddenly she knew he just wasn't running to score. He was running to her.

"A home run! The first of the night, and the Palmetto sheriff's department takes the lead!" The announcer's voice sounded distant, less real than the sound of her own heartbeat as Ryan shook off the backslapping well-wishers and kept moving to where she stood.

Frozen, she waited, unwilling or unable to do anything else. What was about to happen was inevitable, she knew that now. She'd spent a lifetime trying to follow all the rules, to be always be in control of her actions and emotions. But this moment had been building ever since Ryan reappeared in her life. She wasn't going to fight it. She couldn't fight it. She wasn't even sure she remembered why she'd tried.

Which was why when Ryan scooped her into his arms with a celebratory shout, she didn't push him away. Instead, she took all the energy she'd been channeling into keeping him at bay and grabbed on tight. Startled, Ryan looked down at her, a question in his eyes. She didn't have the words to explain something she didn't understand herself. Instead, she kissed him, hard.

His lips tasted of salt and Gatorade, and his neck was sweat slick where her hand pulled his head to hers. Around them was chaos, dirt and noise, but within his arms none of it mattered. There was just her and him and enough sexual energy to light up a dozen ball fields. She should say something, but she didn't know what, and besides, her tongue was too tangled with his to be bothered with something as mundane as language.

It was Ryan who pulled away first, his eyes lit with desire. "I'm going to have to play more ball if that's the reward I can expect for a home run."

The umpire broke in, a knowing grin on his face. "Speaking of playing ball, think you two lovebirds could move out of the way so we can finish the game?"

She should be embarrassed. And maybe she would have been, if not for all the other emotions overwhelming her. Making out in public wasn't her style, especially in front of a set of bleachers packed with her family and friends. Ryan, however, looked completely unrepentant.

"Sorry, Bob." She slid down Ryan's body, feeling exactly how much their kiss had affected him.

"No worries. But seriously, get a room or all the players are going to expect that kind of celebration when they score."

Ryan's grin spread. "You heard the man, let's go." He tugged on her hand and pulled her off the field. She followed, liking the way her hand fit in his. She'd expected him to bring them back to the dugout, but he passed right by it and kept on going.

"Where are we going?"

He pulled her under the bleachers and pressed her up against a painted metal post. "Right here."

"What?" She looked around, seeing no reason for the detour. "Why?"

"So I can do this." Before she could question him further he had covered her mouth with this own, continuing the maddening kiss right where they'd left off. But this time instead of picking her up he used his hands to explore her body, tracing up and down her sides before moving to cup her swollen breasts. "Have I told you how much it's been killing me to keep my hands off you?" he asked, his voice reverberating against her skin.

She squirmed under his touch, the last few months of self denial a dim memory in comparison to the sensory overload of the present moment. "I want to touch you too." Everywhere. And as soon as possible. "But not here."

"No," he agreed, nipping a trail of kisses along her neck, his tongue sneaking under her shirt to trace her collarbone. "Not here." But he showed no signs of stopping, and heaven help her, she didn't want him to. But she also didn't want an audience, right in the middle of a public park. Especially with the entire Palmetto sheriff's department on hand. She was working hard to prove herself, despite her pregnancy. Being found making out under the bleachers like a high school kid probably wouldn't help her cause.

"Home," she whimpered, as his hand delved under her jersey, seeking skin.

"You sure?" he teased. "You were really insistent about wanting to play. Maybe we should go back to the game. The team might need us."

She huffed in frustration. They both knew there were more players than positions, and her pregnancy was more than an adequate excuse to duck out early. "Ryan O'Sullivan, you take me home right now—"

"Or?" He arched a brow, a satisfied smile on his face. Damn him, he knew exactly what he was doing to her. Fine, he could win this one. Or rather, they both could win.

"Or nothing, you jerk. Let's just go. Fast."

He winked, and pulled her toward the parking lot. "Do you think we'd get in trouble if I used the lights and sirens?"

Chapter Fourteen

He'd been joking about the lights and sirens, but he did push the edge of the speed limit. He didn't know what had led to Jessica's change of heart about exploring the physical side of their relationship, but he wasn't risking it changing back again. The whole drive he kept expecting her to tell him to stop, to turn around, to forget the whole thing.

Instead, she sat silently, her fingers anxiously drumming on the armrest while he rethought his decision to live on the outskirts of town. If he'd taken an apartment near the city center they'd be naked by now. At the third red light he muttered a curse against the traffic gods, eliciting a quick smile from Jessica.

"In a hurry to get somewhere, officer?" she asked, eyebrows raised in mock confusion.

He growled, and stomped on the accelerator as the light turned green. Jessica laughed, and his arousal kicked up another notch. By the time he swung the car into his driveway he was starting to wonder if a man could die from sexual tension. Thankfully, it seemed that he wasn't going to find out today. Leaping out of the car he made it to Jessica's door before she managed to release the seatbelt.

"Patience is a virtue you know," she teased, letting him pull her out of the car.

"It's been months, Jessica. I'm all out of patience." To prove his point he pulled her against his body for a long hard kiss, letting her feel exactly how close he was to losing control. Rather than argue she returned the kiss, arching her neck to give him better access to her mouth. Damn, she killed him with the way she melted under his touch. If she was this responsive to a kiss, how much more passionate would she be in his bed?

But first, they had to get inside. Keeping one arm wrapped around Jessica he somehow managed to blindly shove the key in the lock and open the door. Once inside he kicked it shut and put both hands to work. He quickly yanked her shirt over her head, only to realize he still had the tank top and her bra to go. "You are wearing way too many clothes," he growled against her neck as he tugged a strap off her shoulder. "I'm going to let the dog out, and when I get back I want you naked and in my bed."

"I'm all sweaty," she protested, even as she squirmed restlessly against him. "I should shower first."

"Fine." He spun her around in his arms and gave her a little push toward the bathroom. "That works too."

Her eyes widened, but she didn't argue. He heard the water start as he sent Goldie out to romp in the yard and his blood heated as he pictured her naked and wet body.

But when he entered the bathroom he found her waiting for him, still fully clothed, and when he reached for her tank top she backed away, hesitancy crossing her face.

"What is it? Do you need me to stop?" Dear God, it might kill him, but he would if she asked him to. He cared about her too much to ruin things by pushing too hard.

"No, it's just…" Her face flushed and she looked over his shoulder at an invisible spot on the wall. "I don't look like I did, when we were together before." Her hand moved protectively to her belly. "I'm—"

"Stunning." He supplied. "Gorgeous. Sexy as hell." He reached out and placed his hand over hers. "Seriously, Jessica, you're an incredibly beautiful woman who is carrying my child. That makes you more attractive, not less."

She looked up, desire warring with doubt in her eyes. "I don't know…"

"I know. Let me show you." He stroked his hand up her body, lingering over her taut nipple. "Let me show you how much you turn me on." He slid his other hand under her top, sliding it up to reveal her rounded belly. "Let me show you how much I want you."

Wordlessly, she grabbed the hem of her shirt. At first he thought she was going to pull it back down, to stop things right there. Instead, she tore it off in one triumphant motion, and then, eyes bright with need, released the clasp on her bra, letting it fall to the floor. A second later she'd pushed off her remaining clothes and stood before him nude and even more perfect than he'd remembered.

"My God, you're incredible."

Removing his own clothes in record time he pulled her into the shower. Jessica laughed as the spray caught him in the face, and he laughed too, the earlier tension receding. "Turn around."

"Why?"

"So I can wash your back." He picked up a bar of soap and rubbed it, letting the lather fill his hands. Jessica grinned in understanding, and turned, giving him a whole new view to appreciate.

He took his time, exploring every inch of her perfect body with his soap-slicked hands while the water ran over them both. Never one to be passive, Jessica eventually turned and grabbed the soap, a wicked smile on her face. "My turn."

No arguments from him on that, but he wasn't turning his back. He wanted to watch her while she touched him. Her long dark hair streamed down over her breasts, and her skin was rosy from the heat of the shower. She was a goddess, and she was his.

Bracing himself, one hand on the cool tile, the other on the glass shower door, he let her have free rein. When they'd come together the first time it had been a rush of lust and need. Amazing, but over way too fast. This time he was going to savor every single moment.

At least, that was the plan before she started stroking and touching, her hands gliding and teasing, finding erogenous zones he didn't know he had. Only when he was on the verge of exploding did he stop her. Shutting the water off he lifted her hot, slippery body into his arms and headed for the one place he'd wanted her since the very beginning.

For the last few months he'd enjoyed having her in his life but tonight, he'd have her in his bed.

Jessica clutched at Ryan's shoulders as he carried her through the doorway to his room. She hadn't been in there since that the day she'd moved in. She'd thought she had been turned on then, but that had been nothing compared to the inferno raging inside her now. Everywhere her skin touched his she burned, the heat surging through her and then pooling where she needed him most.

The sheets were a cool relief, momentarily easing the fever inside her and promising the wait for satisfaction was nearly over. Ryan positioned himself beside her, his dark hair curling in wet ringlets against his forehead. "Are you sure?" he asked, his voice taut with tension. "Because once we start it's going to be damned hard to stop."

"I'm not going to ask you to stop." She couldn't if she wanted to. Every part of her wanted—no, *needed* this. She needed the release, to forget all the stress of her pregnancy and her career. To feel truly alive instead of like she was just existing. She'd spent so long denying herself, trying to prove herself in school, at the academy, to the department, she'd almost forgotten who she really was.

But Ryan wouldn't let her forget. And so when he reached for her, she didn't hold anything back. All the fears and the doubt melted away as she opened herself, rising up to meet him. Just like before, they fit together as if they'd been made for each other, each instinctively knowing exactly how to please the other. But this time, she didn't let herself dismiss the concept as a schoolgirl fantasy. Instead, she embraced the hope that they could make things work even as she embraced his body.

Because despite her best intentions, she loved him.

The realization, coupled with the sensations pulsing through her, pushed her right over the edge., Clinging to him for dear life, her body shook with the force of her release and left her breathless. Above her, Ryan tensed as his own climax pounded through him, her name on his lips.

It was perfect.

And utterly terrifying.

To her mortification, tears filled her eyes. Ryan, still braced above her, frowned in concern.

"What is it? Did I hurt you? Or the baby?"

She shook her head, reaching up to swipe the traitorous moisture away. "It's just hormones," she lied. "You know how pregnant women get."

He stilled her hand and traced a finger across her damp cheek. "I know exactly one pregnant woman—you. And you don't cry for no reason. Don't shut me out, Jessica. Not now. Not after this." He rolled off her and pulled her into his side, cradling her body against his larger one. His hand gently stroked up and down her back, as if soothing a frightened animal. "Now tell me, what's wrong? If I hurt you, I'm sorry. But I need to know what happened, so I can do things differently next time."

Next time. Here she was having an existential crisis and he was planning their next romp in the sack. It was so stereotypical it would be funny if she wasn't in the middle of a panic attack. Despite everything, she found herself chuckling.

"First you're crying, now you're laughing? Lady, talk to me. Tell me what's going on."

She sighed. "You didn't hurt me. In fact, it was amazing." That much was true.

He sighed, a satisfied smile on his face. "Amazing, huh? Then why the tears?"

Damn, he wasn't going to drop this. And she wasn't going to lie to him, not any more than she already had. Keeping the information about her inheritance a secret was already eating her up inside. Maybe once she'd said the rest of it, he could talk her out of it, tell her how ridiculous she was being.

"It's just… I think I'm falling in love with you." Her voice cracked, and another tear fell.

Ryan blinked slowly, and then he laughed. His body shook with it, vibrating the bed underneath them.

"It isn't funny!" She elbowed him, not quite accidentally, as she sat up. "I know it's probably just the pregnancy hormones, or the orgasm talking, or something. But you don't have to laugh at me!" Angry at him, and at herself, she tried to get out of the bed. If she was going to make an idiot of herself she could at least do it fully clothed.

Ryan stopped her, pulling her against him. "I'm not laughing at you. Really, I'm not."

She rolled her eyes. "Oh no?"

He turned her so they were facing each other. "No," he repeated, his face serious now. "I mean, I'm not laughing at your feelings, anyway."

"What then?"

"I'm laughing at how you made falling in love sound so terrible, like it's a diagnosis of a terminal disease or something."

"Isn't it?" she muttered, even as she felt some of her earlier tension melting under his touch.

"I hope not. But if so, I guess you caught it from me."

"Wait, what?" She searched his eyes for any sign that he was teasing her, and found none.

"I'm saying, if you'll stop freaking out long enough for me to say it, that I love you. I have for a while now. I just was waiting for you to catch up."

Her mouth dropped open. He loved her? "And you don't think that's a big deal?" He was talking about love as if he was discussing what color to paint the living room or what brand of trash bags to buy.

"Of course it's a big deal. But in a good way. It's not supposed to make you cry."

"But this wasn't the plan," she sputtered, her mouth not quite caught up to her brain. "This was supposed to be temporary. Business. Not—"

"A relationship? Honey, you're the one who insisted on all that. Not me."

Her head spun. Yes, she'd known he was attracted to her, that they had chemistry. And yes, he'd talked about seeing where their marriage went. But love? Love changed everything. She'd always known exactly what needed to be done, and how to do it. But love? A relationship? She didn't have a clue what to do with that. So she did the only thing that made sense, and the one thing she hated most of all. She asked for help.

"So what do we do now?"

Ryan grinned. "Well…"

Jessica smacked his chest in frustration, but there was the smallest hint of a smile on her face.

Good. Seeing her cry killed him, especially when it was because of him.

"Men! Is that all you ever think about?"

"No—sometimes we think about food. Which is probably a better idea anyway. Then after we eat we can—"

"Talk," she said, cutting him off before he could suggest a more pleasurable way to pass the time. "We need to talk about what all this means."

He sighed. Talking didn't sound like anywhere near as much fun. "Anyone ever tell you you're bossy?"

"All the time. Now come on, you said you were going to feed me."

Obviously being in love hadn't made her any less the forthright woman he'd come to know. A good thing, as far as he was concerned. He loved that she was feisty, that she didn't let anyone take advantage of her, even him. "Fine." He stood, not bothering to do more than pull on a pair of jeans that were hanging on a chair. "Soup and sandwiches okay?"

She averted her eyes as he dressed, staring at the wall somewhere above his head. "Um, that sounds good. Just give me a minute to get dressed."

"I think it's a bit late for modesty, don't you? We're married, you're carrying my child and we just had the world's most amazing sex."

She grinned. "Now who's saying it was amazing?" But his words had the desire effect. Her shyness gone, she pulled off the sheet that had been covering her and stood, making him wish he'd been a bit less insistent on eating. The sight of her naked body couldn't help but reawaken a whole other kind of hunger, one that was much more fun to satisfy.

Jessica noticed his obvious arousal and shook her head. "Down, boy. Lunch, then conversation."

"And then...?" He waggled his eyebrows in what he hoped was an appealingly suggestive manner.

"Maybe. If you can control yourself while we eat."

He'd be on his best behavior if it meant a repeat of what they'd just done. He could spend all day—for several days—making love to her and it wouldn't be enough. He was going to need a lifetime to get his fill. And for the first time, he had real hope that he might get exactly that. Hearing Jessica admit she loved him was quite possibly the best moment of his life, even if the words had been said through tears. She might be terrified at the idea of making their marriage the real deal, but he had enough certainty for both of them. There was no way he was going to let her slip away again.

First he let the dog back in, giving her a good

petting to make up for ignoring her earlier, then put together two sandwiches while Jessica put a pot of soup onto the stove. While it warmed he dug around in the fridge and found the pickles she favored and added a few to her plate. "Tea?"

"Please."

He poured two glasses of sweet tea and joined her at the kitchen island where she'd filled their soup bowls. They ate in silence, Jessica apparently not quite ready for that conversation she'd insisted they needed to have. When the dishes were rinsed and stacked in the dishwasher and she still hadn't said anything, he decided he'd better take the lead. The sooner they discussed whatever she was worried about the sooner they could do other things. Naked things.

"So, spill it."

She flinched. "What do you mean?"

Man, she was more nervous than he'd realized. Was the thought of a relationship with him really that scary? "You know, there are worse things than being in love with your husband. Some people would actually consider it a good thing—especially when your husband's head over heels for you."

She made a face. "I'm guessing those people got a chance to figure out their feelings before the wedding, not afterward."

"Fair enough." He moved in closer, careful not

to crowd her while she was in this mood. "We did things a bit out of order but that doesn't have to change the end result."

"I don't know. I mean, here we are, about to be a family, and we've never even been on a date."

Was that what was bothering her? "Fine, so let's do that."

She blinked. "Do what?"

"Date. We can go to the movies, dinner, whatever you want."

She smiled. "You'd do that?"

"What, spend time with my beautiful wife? Yeah, I think I could manage to suffer through," he drawled.

She smacked his arm, and he grabbed her hand, pulling her into his arms. Snuggling close, she rested her head on his chest. Her inhaled, taking in the honey-apple scent of her shampoo, and tried to find the right words. "In all seriousness, in case you haven't noticed, I'd do pretty much anything for you."

She looked up at him, her eyes wide. "Why?" She wasn't fishing for compliments—Jessica didn't play games like that. She honestly wanted to know. So he told her.

"Because I love you. And before you ask why again, there are a million reasons. I love that you face down every challenge that comes your way, and never even consider backing down. I love that you are close to your family but don't let them dictate how you live your life. I love that you are brave, and smart and most of all, how honest you are. Like tonight—even though it scared you, you were up-front with me about your feelings. So yeah, I love you, and I count myself very lucky to have you in my life."

She stiffened in his arms and for a moment he thought she was going to argue. But she shook off whatever it was she'd been about to say, and pulled him down for a kiss. It seemed he'd been good after all, and it was time for his reward.

Chapter Fifteen

They spent the rest of the weekend making love. Well, that and eating. She *was* pregnant after all, and her appetite had become something of a running joke between them. Ryan had more than once asked if she was sure she wasn't hiding a litter in there as no single child could possibly require that much sustenance. She'd have been angry, but he had a point. She did eat an ungodly amount. But the doctor said her weight gain was within normal for a first pregnancy, so she wasn't going to worry about it.

"Want another burger?" Ryan asked as he flipped a sizzling patty on the grill.

The smoky smell of the meat tempted her, but she was full to bursting from the one she'd already had, plus baked beans and coleslaw. "No thanks, I'm stuffed."

"Too full for ice cream later?" he teased. "That's a shame, I bought your favorite kind."

She stuck her tongue out at him. "I'll find room. I just need a little time to digest." She stretched out her legs along the deck steps where she was playing a half-hearted game of fetch with Goldie. "And thanks for cooking. Again." He was by far the better cook and had taken over most of the meal prep duties.

"Hey, my reasons are purely selfish. I figure if I feed you well you'll have more energy for later." The heat in his eyes left no doubt as to what she'd need that energy for. Not that she was complaining. Her body was sore in all the right places, but she'd never felt so relaxed, so at peace. No doubt there would be challenges in the future as they adjusted to parenthood, but knowing she'd have Ryan by her side not just as a co-parent but as her husband, by her side forever, made it all seem so much less impossible than it had just a few days ago.

Drowsy from the sun, the meal and a serious lack of sleep, she laid her head on the stair railing and let her eyes drift closed. Goldie, accepting that their ball game was over, agreeably lay down on the bottom step, her head a warm weight on Jessica's feet.

When the doorbell rang, interrupting the droning of the bees and the soft hiss of the grill, she forced herself upright.

"Don't," Ryan said, turning down the burners. "You rest, I'll get it."

She eased back down, sending him a smile of gratitude. "Thanks."

"No problem." She watched him jog toward the gate that connected the backyard to the front, enjoying the view, before closing her eyes again. Maybe she'd just take a little nap while he finished with the dinner clean up. She was right at that delicious space between half-awake and full-on sleep when she felt a shadow over her.

Looking up, she found Ryan with a large envelope in his hand, eyebrows furrowed in confusion.

"What is it?" she asked, but she already knew, her stomach sinking as dread washed over her. How stupid of her to let him answer the door when she knew this was on its way. But then, she'd been expecting it to come by regular mail, not a delivery service.

"You tell me." He sat beside her and handed it over. "I had to sign for it—a courier brought it from that big shot legal firm with all the billboards. He apologized for taking so long, said it was supposed to have been delivered Friday. He said you were expecting it."

She took the envelope, marveling that something that had seemed so important, so monumental, could be contained in such a small package. Just paper and ink, and yet it had the power to change her life.

"Jessica, why were you expecting legal papers? What's going on? I know we said the marriage was temporary, but you agreed to wait until the baby was old enough for daycare before ending things. If those are divorce papers…" Something that sounded very much like fear thickened his voice.

"No, of course they aren't divorce papers."

He scrubbed a hand over his face, wiping sweat from his forehead despite the mild September weather. "Man, I'm sorry for jumping to conclusions like that. It's just I've waited so long, hoping you'd feel what I do, and I thought maybe…" He laughed, "Obviously the lack of sleep has made me stupid. I know you wouldn't keep anything important like that from me."

Guilt turned the meal she'd eaten into tar in her stomach, heavy and awful and impossible to dislodge. She opened her mouth, but no words came out. How could she explain to him that she had done exactly that? No, she hadn't filed for divorce, but she'd kept secrets. She'd fully intended on taking the inheritance money and leaving. She still could.

Except she couldn't imagine anything worse than living without him.

Ryan stroked a strand of hair from Jessica's too-white face. Either he'd really hurt her feelings, or he'd worn her out more than he'd realized over the last two days. "Hey, I didn't mean it. Forgive me, okay?"

She slowly shook her head. "No. I mean, there's nothing to forgive. This isn't on you. It's on me."

His hand dropped. "What are you talking about?" Had he been right about her wanting a divorce? Even if he had, surely she wouldn't want it now, right? Not after she'd admitted she loved him. Hands shaking, he picked the letter up. "What's in this, Jessica? What's got you so upset?"

"It's financial paperwork." She laughed, a dull, lifeless sound full of irony and regret. "So I can access my trust."

"A trust? Like, money?" None of this made any sense. They'd talked about how tight it would be for her to live on a cop's salary as a single mom. Never had she said anything about having money socked away somewhere. Money, or a lack of it, was why she'd been living with her mother, why she'd needed scholarships for school. When had that changed?

"Yeah, a lot of money, actually." She smiled, but it fell flat, never reaching her eyes. "I inherited it from my grandmother a while back, but I don't get access to it until the birth of my first child."

"Oh. Wow." He tossed the idea around in his head, and found he didn't care. He almost dropped the subject and went back to the grill, but something niggled at the back of his brain.

Jessica had rejected his initial proposal of marriage. It was only when he'd pointed out the financial benefits that she'd agreed to the idea. But that didn't make sense—not when she knew she had a big chunk of cash coming as soon as the baby was born. If this inheritance was as big as she'd implied, then she must have had another reason to say yes to him. What was it? And why did she look so miserable now? They said money couldn't buy happiness but it usually didn't make people this actively miserable either.

"There's something else, isn't there? Something you aren't telling me." As soon as he said the words he saw the guilt on her face. Hell, how bad could it be?

"It's just, Grams had some stipulations. That's why there's been so much paperwork. This has been processing for ages."

"What kind of stipulations?"

"I have to prove that I'm married in order to get the money."

He froze. "And you knew this when I proposed? Is that why you agreed to marry me, so you could get your inheritance?"

She bit her lip and nodded.

"And when you got it? What were you going to do then?" She didn't answer, she didn't need to. His blood heated, but this time the fire was fueled by anger, not lust. "You were going to leave, weren't you? Everything we agreed to, raising the baby together, staying together for a year, you didn't mean any of it. You were going to take Grandma's cash and leave." How could he have been so dumb? He'd thought he was being smart, convincing her to marry him, coming up with a plan to raise the baby, biding his time until she realized her feelings for him so they could build a future together…and all along she'd had her own plan—one that didn't involve him. She'd played him for a fool, and he had let her do it. Furious, he shoved off the step and headed inside. He needed to get away from her before he said something he regretted.

He let the back door slam behind him, only to hear it open again as Jessica followed him in. Goldie's nails clicked on the hardwood floor as she joined them, sensitive enough to pick up on the tension in the air, even if she didn't understand the storm brewing between her owners.

"Ryan, wait. Please."

He stopped, turning slowly to face her. "What, Jessica? Is there something else you haven't been honest about? Any other lies I should know about?"

"I never lied to you, Ryan."

He shook his head. "No, I guess you didn't. But you sure as hell weren't honest with me." He grabbed his keys.

"Where are you going?"

He tried not to hear the tears in her voice. This was his time to be upset, not hers. "I don't know."

"When will you be back?"

He shrugged. He didn't have a plan. Goldie snuffled his hand, looking for an invitation to go with him. "Sorry, girl, not this time."

"Please, Ryan, don't go. I know I should have told you, but this doesn't have to change anything. It doesn't have to change how we feel about each other. I love you, Ryan. You have to believe that."

A sad sort of chuckle forced its way past the lump in his throat. "I wish I could. But how can I? How can I believe anything you say, when you've been hiding something like this for months now? You had so many chances to tell me, and you didn't." He opened the front door and then paused. "And you know what? If you had told me from the start, I would have understood. I would have helped you get the money. I just wouldn't have wasted my time falling in love with you."

She was crying when he closed the door. And damned if that didn't hurt him more than his own broken heart.

Watching Ryan walk out of the house, out of her life, was like having a body part ripped off. It physically hurt—more than when she'd broken her leg on her brother's skateboard as a kid, more than when the drunk had fallen on her at the bar, more than the stupid Braxton Hicks contractions she'd started having recently.

More than losing her dad.

Until now, losing her father had been the worst thing that had ever happened to her. First, when her parents split up and he'd left, and then again when he'd died. She'd thought nothing could ever hurt as much as the hole his death had ripped in her heart. But the pain of losing Ryan was every bit as sharp. It didn't make sense—she and Ryan had only had a few days to truly explore what they meant to each other. But somehow, discovering love and then having it taken away in such a short time didn't diminish the effect, it heightened it.

And the worst part was that it was her own stupid fault. She could have said no to the inheritance and Ryan's proposal and just seen what happened naturally. Or she could have told him about it, and let him decide if he still wanted to marry her, knowing she was doing it only for the money.

Only that would have been a lie too.

She'd put plenty of energy into pretending otherwise, but the truth was, she'd had feelings for Ryan from the start. It had just been easier to call it chemistry, or hormones, or plain old lust than to accept that she might have honest-to-goodness emotions tied up in their complicated relationship. How broken was she that she'd pushed away the most perfect chance at a family she could imagine? Was she really that afraid of putting her trust in someone? Did she need to be in control that badly?

Sinking to the cold tile floor she knew the answer was yes. She'd been more comfortable with planning a life as a single mother than the uncertainty of trying to form a family with Ryan, had chosen predictability over a chance at true happiness. "Goldie, that's messed up."

The faithful dog's tail thumped on the ground at the mention of her name. She was a good dog, and great emotional support, but not much of a conversationalist. And Jessica needed to talk this through, to hear someone tell her it would be okay. Because right now, it was hard to imagine how it could be.

Cassie, after Jessica made her promise not to say anything to Alex, led the rescue team, showing up at the front door only minutes after getting Jessica's tearful request. Dani and Sam arrived shortly after, the former carrying ice cream and the latter with two big boxes of pizza. Soon the kitchen was filled with chatter and curse words and the aroma of tomatoes and oregano. Accepting the plate of food Dani pretty much forced on her, Jessica sat at the table and let herself feel grateful for the bond she had with these women, knowing that if anything could mend the sharp pieces of her broken heart it was the friendship they shared.

"Jessica, I can't tell you how sorry I am," Dani apologized for the umpteenth time. "I should have warned you that the paperwork might come via courier."

"You had no way of knowing, and even if you had, it wouldn't have changed the end result—not really. I couldn't have hidden the paperwork from him forever. The truth was bound to come out."

"Still—"

"Stop it. You've been an incredible help. I wouldn't have even known how to get access to my trust without you there to translate all that legalese into English. No, the only person at fault here is me. I betrayed his trust, and he can't forgive that." Heavy mozzarella curdled in her stomach. "And I don't blame him."

"Well I do," Sam argued, the pretty blonde's fair skin flushed with indignation. "You were scared. You two barely knew each other, and you did what you thought was best to protect yourself and the baby. He needs to understand that your motives were good, even if it wasn't the right decision."

"And I think he will, in time." Cassie's was the calming voice of reason, her posture relaxed as she petted Goldie. "You blindsided him, and he reacted strongly. But if he loves you he's going to be just as miserable as you are over this. You just have to give him some time to realize that holding on to a grudge doesn't help either one of you. Sometimes men can be slow that way."

Jessica shook her head. "I don't know. Remember, I'm the one that kept denying what was going on between us. He was up-front right from the beginning, but I pushed him away." She shoved her pizza away, her appetite gone. "Why did I do that?"

"Because if you pushed him away, he couldn't choose to leave." Dani's matter-of-fact pronouncement had Jessica's head whipping toward her.

"What do you mean?" Could it be that stupidly simple?

Dani shrugged. "You were afraid of being let down, of being left alone like your mother. So you just never let him in. The whole 'you can't lose what you never had' thing."

The truth of the young lawyer's words packed a punch, stealing Jessica's breath as she flashed back on every interaction she'd had with the men she'd been involved with. In high school she'd been too busy with softball practice and track team to date. In college she'd dated a man she'd known was going to move away—a planned escape, a clean ending with no hurt feelings or entanglement. And in the academy she'd used her focus on her career to hold everyone at arm's length. The ice queen, they'd called her. Only Ryan had managed to break through the walls she'd so carefully put up. And even still, she'd walked away after their one-night stand, unwilling to even try to make things work. If he hadn't ended up taking a job in Paradise, if she hadn't gotten pregnant…and even then, even after agreeing to marry him, she'd found a way to sabotage things.

Ryan was right to be furious with her. Hell, she was furious with herself. She'd let her unresolved feelings about her father torpedo their chance at happiness. Now the only question was, what was

Ryan going to do about it? She was a realist—their romance was over. But would he stick to their initial agreement, or was she about to find herself pregnant and alone?

It was past midnight when Ryan found himself sitting in his own driveway staring at his front door. He was tired, he was pissed off and he just wanted to crawl in bed until his next shift. But he needed to deal with Jessica first. Walking out hadn't been a very mature reaction, but he'd been too upset to care. Hell, he was still upset, but even as angry and hurt as he was, he knew it wasn't fair to Jessica to leave her in the dark about what came next.

If only she'd shown him the same courtesy.

But she hadn't. She'd let him think they were working together toward a common goal when all along she'd been using him. For money.

It was that last part that hurt the most. Money was why his mother had married his stepfather so quickly. Money was why his stepfather had been so insistent on pushing him toward a law degree rather than the police academy. And now he knew Jessica had chosen money over a real chance at a relationship, that she'd cared more about her inheritance than about being truthful with him.

And that he couldn't get past.

Part of him almost would rather she have cheated. Better to lose her to a flesh and blood rival than the cold seduction of cash.

The street was dark but there was a light shining in the kitchen window. He'd half hoped she'd be asleep, but given the number of night shifts they worked they were both night owls. Something he'd heard might come in handy when the baby came.

It was his concern for the baby that allowed him to keep his emotions in check when he found her sitting at the kitchen table, her feet tucked up under her as she absently stirred a cup of tea. "I'm sorry I walked out like that," he announced.

Startled, she stared at him for a minute. "You're apologizing to me? I'm the one who's sorry."

"You should be." He didn't want her to think otherwise. "Don't get me wrong, I'm still angry as hell, but that doesn't excuse my reaction."

"Oh." She looked down into her mug, as if searching for answers in the steaming liquid. "So now what?"

He blew out a frustrated breath. "I honestly don't know. I'm angry, Jessica. And hurt. I trusted you, and you betrayed that trust, so on top of all that, I feel stupid for believing in you. And I don't like feeling that way."

She nodded slowly, her face expressionless. "I understand. I can be gone tomorrow. And I'm sure we can get the marriage annulled. Dani would know the details on that."

"Damn it, Jessica, I'm not kicking you out." He paced the kitchen, almost wishing he was that big of a jerk. It would certainly make things easier. "And I'm not going to annul the marriage. Yet," he added. "If I do that before the baby is born, you'll lose out on your inheritance. I'm a lot of things, Jessica, but I'm not spiteful. I thought you knew me better than that. But I guess if you did, you'd have told me the truth in the beginning."

She flinched at his words, but he didn't let that keep him from saying what needed to be said. "You can stay—for now. We'll go back to our original agreement, a marriage on paper only, and just until the baby is old enough for daycare."

"I appreciate that."

"I'm not doing it for you. I'm doing it for the baby."

"I never meant to hurt you." Her voice was strong, but he could hear the pain beneath the pride.

"I believe you." He did. But the damage was done, and it didn't hurt any less than if she'd planned it. "But I can't have a relationship without trust. You didn't trust me. And now I can't trust you."

"So that's it?" Her eyes filled, their rich brown

depths drowning in a whirlpool of emotion. "You're giving up on us?"

He'd spent the last few hours asking himself that same question, but hearing it on her lips reignited the anger he'd tried to tamp down. She didn't have a right to ask that of him, not after how patient he'd been, how hard he'd tried. He'd spent the last few months waiting and hoping and wondering, doing everything he could to convince her to give their marriage a real shot. She was the one that had thrown their chance at happiness away, not him.

So he let the anger coursing through him go cold, cold enough to numb his still bleeding heart. Because as much as he loved her, he wouldn't set himself up for that kind of pain again. If she wanted the money so badly, she could have it. But she wouldn't have him.

"You sold out our chance at love when you decided cash was more important than honesty. I just hope it was worth it."

Without looking back, he headed to his room and shut the door on her and whatever fantasy of a family he'd built up in his head.

Chapter Sixteen

Category 2 Hurricane
Winds of 96-110 MPH
Expect flooding, power outages and flying debris
Mandatory evacuation for all barrier islands

Hurricane Nova was barreling toward Paradise Isle, sneaking in on the last day of hurricane season, but it was the maelstrom of her life that was preoccupying Jessica's thoughts.

It had been thirteen weeks and three days since she'd realized she was in love with Ryan. And after their big blow up, every minute had been an agony of polite dismissal. Yes, he asked her how her day was, and yes, he went to the doctor's appointments with her. He'd even participated in the childbirth classes the hospital provided. But there were no more spontaneous conversations, no more casual touches. Now when he went to the grocery store he stuck to a list rather than sneaking in little surprises he thought she might like.

To his credit, he never brought up her dishonesty, nor said an angry word. He was a model of a gentleman. The perfect roommate.

And it was killing her.

She'd thought their fight the day the trust fund paperwork arrived was the worst thing that could happen. But this cold civility was so much worse. Every day she had to see him, and know she couldn't have him—not physically, and not as the true friend and partner he'd become in the early days of her pregnancy. Every day she was reminded of what she'd had and then lost. People said that time healed all wounds, but how could it when the scar was constantly being ripped open?

Only once had she gotten a glimpse of the old Ryan, the one she'd fallen in love with, the one who had loved her too. It had been a brief but powerful moment, when, in a cramped exam room, her belly covered in goo, they'd squinted together at a grainy black-and-white picture hoping that this time the baby would cooperate and they'd finally be able to find out if the baby she was carrying was a boy or a girl.

Without thinking she'd clutched Ryan's hand, her heart pounding as they waited. Back in her second trimester, when their already stubborn unborn child refused to uncross his or her legs, Ryan had claimed he didn't care, as long as the baby was healthy, but she knew he wanted a son to carry on his late father's name. She wanted that for him. So when, after all the waiting, the technician announced it was a boy she'd impulsively pulled him into a hug. For half a second he'd returned the embrace before remembering himself and pulling away. After the appointment she'd wanted to celebrate, to enjoy the moment together, but the wall he'd so carefully built was already back up between them.

Since then she'd been careful not to let herself forget that theirs was a business arrangement, nothing more. Her heart wasn't strong enough to take the pain of constant rejection otherwise. Even still, it was a dull ache, always with her. Her friends had thrown her a shower, and were encouraging her to look forward to the birth of her son. But how could she, when counting down the days to her due date just reminded her that her time with Ryan was running out?

As hard as it was to live with him she couldn't imagine how hard it would be to leave. She'd grown accustomed to hearing him sing off-key in the shower in the morning, to seeing his dirty running shoes on the front step when she got home. They might not be a normal family, but they fit together. Moving out was going to be like losing a part of herself.

But she couldn't think about that now. The baby was due in three weeks, and that had to be her focus. That, and her job. She'd moved to mostly desk work as her duty belt had gotten too difficult to wear for hours on end, but today, it was all hands on deck to enforce evacuation orders. She and the other deputies were tasked with making sure everyone knew about the warning and was able to get to safety well ahead of the storm. Those without transportation were being given free bus tickets, but even so, not everyone was willing to go. Legally she couldn't force anyone to evacuate, but she'd do her best to convince any stragglers it was in their best interest to move inland. A few hours from now she'd be doing that herself. Only a skeleton crew would stay at the station, and once the winds reached forty miles per hour all first responders would be off the roads, leaving those who refused to evacuate on their own until the storm passed. A harsh reality she had no problem pointing out if it would change a few old-timers' minds about riding it out.

She'd finished canvassing her assigned residential streets and was now tackling the downtown businesses. Many were already boarded up, their owners gone. Of course, most of them would have flood and storm insurance, making it easier to leave. Some of the residents didn't, and so stayed in a mistaken belief they could somehow protect their property by being there. But nothing and no one could win when the battle was with Mother Nature.

Halfway down the block she was surprised to see the Sandcastle Bakery still in operation, a hand-lettered open sign stuck to the aluminum storm shutters that covered the windows. Ducking in out of the rising wind she found Grace Keville packing boxes of baked goods.

"Grace! Don't tell me you're staying?" The older woman didn't strike her as the foolhardy type.

"Oh, no. Lester is picking me up in a little while, and we've got a hotel reserved in Kissimmee. Figure once the storm passes we might hit the theme parks, make a day of it."

Jessica smiled. Leave it to Floridians to find a way to enjoy a hurricane. "Still, you're cutting it close. Curfew starts in an hour."

"Oh, I know." Grace closed up one box and started packing another. "We'll be gone by then. But I figured we'd drop off some goodies at the sheriff's office and the fire department before we go. They're just going to go stale otherwise. And some coffee, of course. I've had enough of you deputies in here complaining about the stuff they brew at the station to know my special roast might be appreciated."

"You are an angel. An honest-to-goodness angel." She eyed a sugar-crusted apple fritter. "If I'd known you were going to be supplying the refreshments I might have volunteered to stay myself."

"Oh no!" Grace shook her head, her perfectly coiffed silver hair barely moving. "You know, they say storms can bring on labor, something about the barometric pressure. You need to be somewhere safe on the mainland. But," she winked, "I wouldn't want you to make that drive on an empty stomach." She slipped the fritter Jessica had been eyeing into a small paper bag and handed it to her. "For the road."

"Thank you." Jessica's stomach grumbled in anticipation. "Don't suppose you have any decaf to go with it?"

"Of course, help yourself. It's the urn on the left, the one with the red spout." She paused, "Oh, I forgot to ask if you want anything for that handsome husband of yours. What does he like?"

"Ryan? He's staying at the station. My mom and I are going to make a girl's night of it—she's already at the hotel." She tried to keep her voice light, but Grace's eyes narrowed in disapproval. "Hmph. Doesn't that silly man know his place is with you during all this? I've half a mind to send my Lester over to tell him so. Wife ready to pop and a storm coming on—he should be right there by your side!"

Secretly, Jessica agreed. But there was no reason for him not to work—she had weeks until the baby was supposed to arrive and her mom would be with her. She'd be perfectly safe so far inland— Orlando wasn't predicted to get more than a bit of rain and a stiff breeze.

She told Grace as much, thanked her for the refreshments, and headed back out. She had a job to do, and no time for old wives' tales, even ones served with a side of pastry.

Ryan parked the patrol car in front of the station, warily eyeing the wall of clouds moving in from the southeast. You couldn't truly predict something as wild as a hurricane, but every indication was that it was going to pack a wallop and Paradise Isle was in the crosshairs. The station had been retrofitted to meet current building codes, and the homes built in the years since Hurricane Andrew would probably be fine. But there were plenty of older homes that were in danger, and of course there was the storm surge to contend with as well. If Nova behaved herself and stayed offshore they shouldn't make out too badly, but a direct hit would mean massive devastation. He'd faced down some bad storms in Miami, and didn't relish seeing that kind of destruction here.

At least Jessica would be safe. He'd insisted she evacuate and their superiors had agreed. He was trying so hard to keep his feelings for her on lockdown, but the way his heart pounded at just the thought of her in danger told the true story. He still loved her. He'd never stopped. He just didn't know what to do about it. His religion preached forgiveness, and his heart agreed. But his pride told him he'd made the right choice in pushing her away.

Or was that just cowardice talking? Was he doing the sensible thing, or was he just afraid of getting hurt again?

Spitting rain chilled his skin as he sprinted across the parking lot into the relative warmth of the station. Most of those who were staying were already there, helping themselves to the contents of a stack of pizza boxes and telling war stories of past storms. The natives, like him, had been through other hurricanes, others had heard stories. All knew the power that was about to be unleashed, and the nervous tension in the room belied their casual tone. But that was how people made it through these kinds of things. A little gallows humor helped keep you sane when the world as you knew it was at risk of being blown into the ocean.

"Hey, O'Sullivan, I thought you'd be on your way to Orlando with my mom and Jessica." Alex crossed the room to him, a bottle of water in one hand and the duty roster in another. "I was just about to tell Jeremy he'd made a mistake on this thing."

"No mistake. I'm here for the duration."

"Seriously?" Alex frowned. "Dude, she's pregnant. Really, really pregnant. Don't you think she needs you?"

"I know how pregnant she is. But you know your sister, she's fully capable of taking care of herself. She said she was fine with me staying."

"Oh hell, she used that word? She said 'fine'?"

Ryan shrugged, and grabbed a slice of pizza for himself. "Yeah, I think so. Why?"

Alex shook his head and laughed, a look of sheer disbelief on his face. "I'd have thought you'd have figured it out by now. When my sister says something is fine it means exactly the opposite.

Her escalation levels are annoyed, angry, totally pissed off and fine. You, my friend, are in deep doggy doo."

"Knock it off. If she'd wanted me to go with her she would have said something."

"Probably." Alex took a swig of water. "Which means you must have already been skating on thin ice." He ducked into an empty office and motioned for Ryan to follow. In the private room his face sobered. "Seriously, are things okay with you guys? I know she doesn't like to talk about personal stuff with the family, but she clams up every time Mama asks how things are going, and it seems like you've always got other plans when she makes family dinner."

Mrs. Santiago's family dinners were a monthly affair, full of Puerto Rican cooking, good-natured teasing and a lot of fun. He'd made it to a few early on, back when he'd thought it was just a matter of time before he and Jessica were a real couple. But ever since telling her it was over he'd managed to excuse himself, volunteering for extra shifts, faking illness, whatever it took. Her mother was too insightful; she'd have been sure to see the painful distance between him and his bride, to ask questions he didn't know how to answer.

"I've just been busy, that's all. And you know how hormonal pregnant women can be."

"Man do I," Alex grimaced. "But that's usually silly stuff. Getting angry because you brought the wrong brand of ketchup or something. But Jessica… She just seems kind of sad lately. Is it the baby, man? Because if there's something wrong—"

"No, he's fine." Ryan smiled at the thought of his son. "Doctor says he's as healthy as can be."

"Good, that's good." He nodded in relief before his expression turned serious. "But listen, I know I gave you a hard time when I found out about you and Jessica. She's my little sister, you know? But you've been good for her, I can see that. So if there's something going on…"

Ryan was torn. On the one hand, Alex was a Santiago, his loyalties would always be to his sister. But damned if he didn't need to talk to someone, and Alex was one of the only married men he'd made friends with since moving to the island. And no one knew Jessica better.

"We've hit a bit of a bumpy spot," he admitted. "She held back something, something she should have told me, and I'm having a hard time getting past it."

"That's tough." Alex spun the water bottle between his hands, thinking. "Is it something that, had you known, would have changed how you feel about her? Or would you still have married her if you knew?"

"I still would have married her," Ryan answered without hesitation.

"Then I guess that's your answer, isn't it?"

"But she didn't trust me enough to tell me—in fact, she deliberately hid it from me. Doesn't that mean something?"

Alex shrugged. "Jessica's not the type that trusts easily. She's all about being independent, solving all her own problems, never asking for help. She's been that way since she was a kid watching our mom get let down time after time. And face it, you two barely knew each other when you got hitched. I get the love at first sight thing, but trust at first sight? Cut her some slack. You'll both be happier for it."

Ryan nodded slowly. Maybe he had been unfair, expecting Jessica to trust him that much that quickly, when so much was at stake. And later, she'd probably been afraid that admitting her deception would push him away—a self-fulfilling prophecy. It wasn't right, but maybe they could find a way to work past it, if she wanted to. "You might have a point."

"Of course I do. Trust is earned, and if I was you I'd start by taking your name off that duty roster and finding her before they close the roads down."

Alex was right. If he wanted to prove to Jessica he had her best interests at heart, he needed to start acting like a real husband, not some schoolboy who'd had his feelings hurt. He needed to go find his wife.

Jessica banged on the locked door of the Paradise Animal Clinic. The shutters were up and the welcome sign was flipped to Closed but she'd seen Cassie's car in the lot and there were lights on in the back. A chorus of barking answered her knock—were the animals the only ones in there? Or was Cassie trying to be a hero?

Jessica had passed right by the clinic during her first patrol of the street, assuming it was empty. She'd gone home, grabbed Goldie and an overnight bag, and was headed for the mainland when she'd spotted Cassie's car.

Worried, she banged again, hard enough to rattle the glass. "Cassie! Are you in there?" Maybe she'd had car trouble and gotten stuck? But surely she would have called someone for a ride.

Worried, she absently rubbed her belly. The Braxton Hicks contractions were getting to be a real pain. Finally, she spotted Cassie coming to the door, smiling as if she didn't have a care in the world. As soon as the door was unlocked Jessica pushed her way in. "What are you doing here!

The bridge will be closing soon, you've got to get out now."

Cassie shook her head, "I'm staying."

Jessica felt her mouth drop. "You've got to be kidding."

"Nope. I've got patients that can't be moved. But don't worry," she added quickly, "this place is built like a vault. Everything is up to the highest code, built to withstand a Cat 4. And I've got generators for power and plenty of water and food. Dad's ridden out plenty of storms here. I'll be fine."

"Does Alex know? And what about the kids?" Surely she wasn't keeping them here during the storm.

"Alex doesn't love the idea, but he knows the building is safe, and since he's staying on the island too he doesn't have much room to complain. And the kids went inland with my parents. They're staying at one of those touristy resorts with mini golf and a wave pool and everything. They'll have a blast."

Jessica nodded, her attention diverted once again to the pain squeezing her insides.

"Are you okay?"

Jessica nodded, waiting for it to pass. "Just Braxton Hicks."

Cassie's brow furrowed. "That seemed pretty intense for a Braxton Hicks contraction."

"I guess being on my feet for so long is making them worse. The doctor said that could happen, and to drink some water and put my feet up."

"And have you been drinking water?" Cassie asked pointedly.

"Um, no." Embarrassed, she shook her head. "I've been so busy..."

"I'll get you some then." She headed for her office. "Want anything else? A snack or something? I've got plenty."

"I'm good." Another pain gripped her, stealing her breath. "Actually, maybe I'll just sit down for a minute, if that's okay."

"Of course." Cassie handed her a cold bottle dripping with condensation. "Are you sure you're okay? Do you want me to call someone? Alex, maybe?"

"No." She eased onto one of the waiting room chairs. "I'll be fine in a minute. I just pushed myself too hard, that's all." She took a sip of water and forced a smile. "See, better already."

"Good."

A sudden shriek of wind whistled under the eaves, and then rain was slapping at the shutters, sounding like some monstrous creature trying to get it. Cassie moved to the one unshuttered window and peered out. "Looks like the first of the rain bands are here—sooner than they predicted. The storm must have picked up speed."

"Which means I need to get out of here." She hefted herself out of the chair and was immediately smacked back down by another wave of pain. "Crap." She leaned over, bracing her hands on the wall as the sensation built and then faded.

"Jessica, I don't think you are in any condition to drive yourself anywhere."

"Well that's too bad." She straightened. "If I wait any longer the bridge will be closed and I'll be stuck here."

Before Cassie could offer an argument, the front door swung open, letting in a torrent of hard pelting rain. Ryan, drenched to the bone, stepped in, his eyes going immediately to Jessica. Behind him was Goldie, her blond fur dark and dripping. "There you are! I've been looking everywhere for you! And when I found Goldie alone in the car—" He cut himself off, out of breath, worry plain on his face. Swiping water from his face he glared at her. "Don't you ever answer your phone?"

Oops. "I'm sorry, I turned it off—my mom calling to ask for an update every five minutes. I planned to turn it back on when I got on the road. Speaking of which, I'd better head out." She shot a warning glance at Cassie, willing her sister-in-law to keep quiet about her contractions. Braxton Hicks were normal, and nothing to worry about.

If she kept saying it, it would be true, right?

Even as she had that thought, another one hit, the pain like a vise clamping down on her entire midsection.

Instantly Ryan was at her side, holding her steady as she breathed through it. "Whoa, what's wrong?" He looked from Jessica to Cassie and back again, his eyes wide with concern.

Unable to speak, she reluctantly nodded at Cassie, giving her permission to share.

"I'm pretty sure she's in labor," Cassie stated. "She's insisting she's not, but I've had two kids and I know what labor looks like. And it's looking like it's going to be a quick one, as fast as the contractions are coming. You need to get her to the hospital right away."

"I can't!" His grip on her arm tightened. "That's why I was calling you. They already closed the bridge. The storm picked up speed and is going to hit much sooner than anyone thought. They're clocking tropical force winds up and down the coast."

"But you're a cop," Cassie argued. "Surely you can get access if it's a medical emergency?"

"I can get past the barriers, sure, but a badge isn't going to stop the car from being blown into the water by a gust of wind. We close that bridge for a reason." He lowered Jessica back onto a chair and planted himself in front of her, hands on his hips in what she thought of as his alpha male cop pose. "So you can't be in labor now. You'll have to wait."

Chapter Seventeen

Ryan knew as he said it how ridiculous he sounded, but he meant those words with all his heart. She absolutely could not be in labor right now. It just wasn't an option.

"What about the family clinic?" Cassie asked. "I know they aren't a hospital, but the doctors there will surely be able to handle things."

Jessica had been staring at him in disbelief, either at the situation or his stupid order to stop having contractions, but she shook her head in answer to Cassie's suggestion. "They evacuated hours ago. They aren't equipped to stay up and running if the power goes out. That's one of the main reasons for the mandatory evacuation—there won't be any medical services running until the winds die down."

"Maybe it's just false labor," he suggested. "Might just fizzle out."

"Maybe," she agreed hopefully, her words nearly drowned out by the roaring of the wind outside. But then her face tightened, and her breath quickened. "Or maybe not. Man, that hurts."

"What are we going to do?" He wasn't sure who he was asking or what answer he expected.

"We're going to have a baby, that's what."

Jessica's face blanched at Cassie's words, and Ryan's knees nearly buckled. "What? You can't be serious."

"Look at her—she's having the baby, right here, right now, hurricane or no hurricane." Cassie pointed to where Jessica was curled over, her knuckles white where they gripped the seat of her chair. "And we've got everything we need. I've delivered lots of babies. Granted, they all had four legs, but the process is the same." Her smile did nothing to calm the fear turning his brain to jelly. But even in his panic he knew a veterinarian was not the same as an obstetrician.

Jessica, putting his thoughts into words, protested. "No way. I'm having a baby, not a litter of puppies."

"I know this isn't ideal." Cassie bent down, putting a hand on Jessica's shoulder, looking her in the eye. "But I've had two children of my own. I know how this goes, and I'm not going to let anything bad happen to my first nephew. You can trust me."

That they didn't have any real choice in the matter was left unsaid.

Another contraction gripped Jessica. Ryan had never felt so helpless in his life. He wanted a way to fix things, a physical enemy to fight. He'd wrestle the storm with his bare hands if it would make a difference. He was armed and trained and completely helpless.

They were out of options.

"Ryan, see if you can put a call into 911, before the circuits get overloaded. We may not be able to get anyone out here now, but at least they'll know what's going on and will send someone out once the winds die down." To Jessica, she offered a smile. "I'm going to go get some blankets and supplies, okay? Let's see if we can't get you a bit more comfortable. It's going to be okay, I promise."

Ryan held on to that assurance as he dialed, needing to believe her. Needing to think something in this drawn-out mess was going to turn out right. He'd messed up with Jessica—he couldn't mess up with his kid.

A hurried conversation with a busy emergency operating didn't offer any new hope. She confirmed that all emergency vehicles had been grounded until the winds receded, and she had no timetable of when that might happen—though she promised to dispatch one in their direction as soon as possible. But until then, that meant they were really and truly on their own.

"They say first labors can take a long time, right?" He wasn't sure if he was asking Jessica or Cassie, but it was the latter woman who answered. "Absolutely," she said cheerfully, pushing a small portable cart piled high with supplies. "My first one lasted days. But," she continued more soberly, "Jessica's contractions are less than five minutes apart. Hopefully we'll just hunker down for a bit and then she can deliver at the hospital like you planned. But if things progress quickly, and they might, we'll be fine."

How she could say that with a straight face he didn't know. But either she was an incredible actress or she truly believed what she was saying. He prayed she was right. And prayed for the storm to turn it's destructive butt around and head back out to sea the way it had come, ASAP. He wanted people, doctors and nurses and a bunch of fancy equipment, to reassure him his wife and baby were okay, because nothing else in his life would ever matter if they weren't.

But the storm didn't care what he wanted. Outside, the winds kept screaming, rattling the metal shutters, while the rain pounded down in waves. Inside, there were no doctors in crisp lab coats, no nurses bustling around telling him what to do. Instead of a fancy hospital bed, Jessica reclined in his lap in a pile of blankets and towels. He did, at least, get the reassurance of a bit of fancy equipment when Cassie wheeled out a portable ultrasound machine. A quick peek revealed that the baby was still head down and doing well. Cassie promised to keep checking, and then attached a sensor to Jessica's finger to record her pulse and oxygen saturation.

All the while, he was focused on Jessica, so small and yet so strong, lying back against his chest. Each contraction seemed longer and stronger than the last, and all he could do was hold her as she panted from exertion, sweat beading on her forehead. How did women tolerate this, generation after generation?

Never again would he be able to think of women as the weaker sex. Not when they were able to do this. Even in the midst of his fear he was in awe of her strength. And if they made it through this he'd spend the rest of his life making sure Jessica knew how proud he was of her.

Jessica had no idea how long she'd been laboring. Time had ceased to be measured in minutes and hours—all she was aware of was contractions. Each time one came she counted down in her head until the pain finally eased and she collapsed back into Ryan's arms again.

"She's in transition now," Cassie said, a tight expectancy in her voice. "She'll want to push soon."

"No," Jessica grunted. Pushing meant having the baby, and she wasn't ready to do that. She might never be ready. She still needed to try to make things right with Ryan. She needed to finish putting together the crib. She needed to get to the hospital! "No pushing."

Cassie chuckled. "When it's time, you won't be able to help it. But don't worry, things are going great." To prove it she placed the ultrasound probe back on Jessica's belly and the swooshing sound of their son's heartbeat filled the room, drowning out the storm and the fear and the pain.

"You can do this," Ryan assured her, his voice thick with emotion. "You are so strong. You can do anything."

Some of his confidence seeped into her, restoring her flagging spirits. She'd known labor could be painful, but she hadn't known how overwhelmingly *big* it would be. Her own power was dwarfed by the surges of pressure sweeping over her. It was like being hit by a rogue wave, the surf sucking her down and tossing her until she didn't know which way was up or if she'd ever escape its pull. Except instead of a single wave she was being pounded over and over again, sure to drown except for Ryan's constant comforting presence.

"Don't leave me," she whispered, her voice hoarse.

"I'm not going anywhere." He gripped her hand harder, as if to assure her of his promise.

She wanted to tell him she didn't mean now, she meant ever. Yes, she needed him there with her while she brought this baby into the world, but she needed him for so much more. For everything. Forever. But pain stole the words before she could say them. "Oh!" was all she managed as she desperately tried to find a better position, one where it didn't feel like her bones were going to split apart. Shifting forward out of Ryan's arms and into a squat, she felt her body pushing without her permission, just as Cassie had predicted.

"Good job, Jessica! You're doing it," the veterinarian-turned-midwife cheered.

She wanted to argue, to say she wasn't consciously *doing* anything, she was just along for the ride. But conversation was beyond her now. She'd become something much more primitive, every instinct focused on breathing and bearing down and getting her baby out…out…OUT!

"I can see the head!"

Without thinking, Jessica reached down and, with Ryan's strong arms supporting her, pushed her baby out into her own hands.

He was wet and wrinkly and had the most enormous eyes and he was the most beautiful thing she'd ever seen in her life. "I did it?" she asked, awe and wonder and disbelief in her voice.

"Hell yeah, you did!" Ryan crowed, peering over her shoulder at the newest member of their family. "Look at him, he's perfect."

"He sure is." Cassie nodded approvingly, tears in her eyes and a relieved smile splitting her face. "You did great, Jessica." She grabbed a clean towel and swapped it out for the one Jessica was still squatting over. "Here, you go. Ryan, let Jessica lean back against you again, okay? She's shaking and we don't want her to drop him. There, that's it. Just keep the little guy on her chest there and we'll wait for the placenta. Or the paramedics, whichever comes first."

Jessica tensed in Ryan's arms. "I have to push that out too, don't I?"

Cassie laughed. "Yes, but don't worry, that's the easy part, I promise. Won't hurt a bit."

Mollified, Jessica went back to getting to know her baby, stroking his still-slick skin, tracing the contours of this little stranger who had been a part of her for so long and was now his very own person. "He's a miracle," she breathed in awe.

"No, you're the miracle," Ryan said, his voice husky. "And I've been an ungrateful fool not to tell you so before."

Her breath caught. Had she heard him right or was she still out of it from the birth? "What are you saying?"

"I'm saying I love you." He snuggled her closer against him, as if hoping to physically keep her in his life. "I never stopped. And I'm sorry for acting like that wasn't enough, like all that other stuff was more important. It wasn't. Can you forgive me?"

Jessica remembered how he'd walked out on her, how he'd ended things almost as soon as they'd begun.

And yet, their love hadn't ever really died. The proof of that was in her arms, alive and well and looking up at her with his father's beautiful brown eyes.

Which was why it was easy, so very easy, to answer his question.

"No, Ryan O'Sullivan, I will not forgive you."

* * *

Ryan's shoulders sagged, the weight of the last few hours nothing compared to the burden of knowing he'd truly, permanently ruined things with Jessica. He never should have brought it up, not now. He had no right to taint this moment with bad memories. "I'm sorry, I shouldn't have asked—"

"That's right, you shouldn't have. Because you have nothing to apologize for." She smiled at him, her face practically glowing with joy. "I can't forgive you when there's nothing to forgive. I'm the one that messed everything up, not you."

"How about you two just agree to start over?" Cassie suggested cheerfully as she covered mother and baby with a worn blue blanket embroidered with yellow paw prints. "Nothing says new beginnings like a birth."

"What do you think, baby boy?" Jessica crooned to the wide eyes of their son. "Think your daddy and I should start over and give you a real family?"

"Pretty sure he said yes," Ryan lied, reaching down to stroke an impossibly small hand.

"Oh, you think so?" Jessica chuckled.

"Absolutely. And you wouldn't want to disappoint him on his birthday, would you?"

"No, I suppose not." She winced, and he looked up at Cassie, fresh fear pulsing through him.

"What's wrong? It thought it was over."

Cassie nodded. "It is, these are just the after pains. They're a normal part of the process, but they can be pretty intense."

"You're telling me!" Jessica shifted in his arms uncomfortably.

"Is there anything I can do?" He couldn't stand to see her in pain. But she shook her head, her toughness impressing him once again.

"No, just stay here with me."

"You couldn't pry me away."

They sat like that, her in his lap and the baby in her arms, for an hour. At some point Ryan had cut the cord with a pair of sterile scissors Cassie handed to him. Shortly after that Jessica delivered the placenta and then Cassie let them be, busying herself with cleaning up and surreptitiously checking on mother and baby every few minutes. Goldie, who'd been relegated to Cassie's office after getting a bit too concerned for her mistress, had been let back out, and after a quick sniff of the newcomer was content to curl up on a borrowed dog bed.

Outside, the wind still blew but instead of roaring like a freight train it whimpered, whining around the eaves. The lights had flickered several times, but so far the power was holding out. They were in their own little bubble, cut off from the outside world but safe and sound. They even had snacks, courtesy of Cassie's hurricane stash. He held a plastic cup of orange juice to Jessica's lips and watched her drink as their son nursed at her breast. "So, what are we going to call him?" They hadn't gotten around to names before the big blowup and after that he hadn't had the heart to discuss it.

"Matthew, after your father."

"Are you sure? We could name him after someone in your family. Or whatever you want." She was the one who had worked so hard to bring him into the world, it seemed only fair to let her have the final say.

"I'm sure. We'll give him my father's name for a middle name. So neither of them is ever forgotten."

Ryan's eyes, which had miraculously remained dry during the birth, suddenly filled. He had never been the type to cry, but something about seeing the past carried into the future, knowing that his son would have that connection with the grandfathers he would never know, was more than he could take. He scrubbed at his eyes with the back of his fist, and changed the subject. "Is there any update on the hurricane?"

Cassie pulled out her phone and tapped the screen. "It certainly sounds like it's calmed down out there. Hopefully the paramedics will be able to get on the roads soon."

As she spoke the faint wail of a siren rose over the sounds of the storm. Never had such a grating sound been so welcome.

"Pretty sure that's the cavalry right now," Cassie exclaimed, racing for the front door. "I'll go wave them down."

Jessica smiled, "It's almost like she's looking forward to kicking us out."

He chuckled. "Yeah, well, I'm more than ready to go. Aren't you?"

Nodding, she gripped the little baby to her chest. "As long as you're going with me."

He kissed her temple, tasting the sweat and strength that had gotten her this far, and whispered, his throat tight with emotion, "Woman, I'd go anywhere with you. In fact, I may never let you out of my sight again."

Chapter Eighteen

True to his word, Ryan had stuck to her side as if glued there, even as hours had turned to days had turned to weeks, Jessica mused, as she gently wrestled their one-month-old son into the world's tiniest white suit. She'd wanted a more traditional baptismal gown but Ryan had insisted they looked too girly, and he'd been such a hands-on, doting father she hadn't had the heart to argue. Truly, the man had been amazing, waiting on her hand and foot while she recovered. He'd insisted on riding in the ambulance when it had taken her and the baby to be checked out at the hospital and hadn't left her side since, until today.

He'd probably be underfoot right now if her mother hadn't physically kicked him out, reminding him that it was bad luck to see the bride before the wedding. He'd protested that they were already married, but her mama had never lost an argument in her life and wasn't going to let such a small technicality beat her now. She'd just muttered something in Spanish and physically closed the door in his face.

Cassie had been allowed in due to her dual roles as matron of honor and godmother. A few more friends were waiting in the church, but the ceremony would be small. A renewal of vows was what they were calling it, but for Jessica it felt like they were finally getting things right. This time they'd make their vows from the heart, with their loved ones surrounding them and no secrets between them.

The whole thing had been her mother's idea. She had a birthday coming up and Jessica had offhandedly asked what she'd like for it. A church wedding had been her only request. It seemed likely the wish was more about witnessing her daughter walk down the aisle than any particular religious hang-ups, but Jessica didn't mind. They'd already reserved the sanctuary for baby Matthew's baptism, so it had been easy enough to convince the priest to perform both ceremonies.

The only added expense had been a new dress. Glancing in the mirror her mother had propped up in the choir's practice room she admired it again. As soon as she'd seen it she'd known it was the one. The skirt was long but light, swirling around her legs with each step she took. The high waist hid the last few pounds of baby weight she needed to shed, and the faux wrap–style bodice, with its deep neckline, was perfect for nursing. Which was good given Matthew was growing like a weed, and had the appetite to prove it.

Dani, the most fashion conscious of her friends, had done her makeup and hair, twisting it up into a loose updo with a few curling tendrils loose around her face. *Not bad for a new mom who hasn't slept in weeks.*

"Is everyone decent?" Alex's voice called from the other side of the door. "Ryan's getting impatient—I'm not sure I can keep him away much longer."

Jessica rolled her eyes. "You're a trained law officer. You can handle it, big brother. Or are you saying he's stronger than you?"

Alex replied with a crude word that was most definitely not appropriate for church.

"Alexander Santiago, have some respect," their mother rebuked. "And tell them to take their places, we'll be right out." Turning to Jessica, she held out her hands. "Here, give the *bebe* to me. Your groom is waiting."

Jessica nestled the tiny tyke in his grandmother's arms, where he instantly settled into a content sleep. "If he wakes up—"

"He won't." She kissed Jessica on the cheek, her eyes beaming with pride. "You look beautiful, *mija*."

"So do you." She was stunning actually, in a plum pantsuit and a new, shorter hairstyle that, although she would never admit to it, had been professionally highlighted. She seemed to grow younger with each grandchild, which hardly seemed fair, given that Jessica felt like she'd aged ten years since Matthew's birth.

"Are you ready?" Cassie asked, nodding to where Jessica was picking at the embroidery on her dress. "You know, you've done this once before, you'd think you'd be past nerves by now."

"It's not nerves, I just hate waiting around." Action was more her style, and after weeks of maternity leave she was getting twitchy. Soon she'd be back at work part-time. They still hadn't quite figured out how that was going to work, but they would sort it out eventually. They'd gotten past bigger obstacles—they'd manage this one too.

Strains of Wagner's wedding march began to

echo through the old wooden church, and Jessica's heart skipped a beat.

After fighting against it for too long it was time to claim her happily-ever-after.

Ryan tugged at his jacket sleeves as he peered down the aisle. He never should have let himself be talked into wearing a tuxedo. It wasn't necessary for such a small, private ceremony, especially since they were already married. But his mother-in-law had insisted, and since the whole thing was her idea—and her birthday present—he'd tried to be a good sport. Now he was hot and itchy and wondering why he'd let himself be pushed around by a woman half his size.

A door opened at the back of the church, a stripe of golden winter sun falling across the polished wooden floor of the church as a late-arriving couple entered the building. Ryan's breath caught as he recognized them. "I don't believe it." He'd sent the invitation but hadn't received a response and honestly hadn't expected one. Yet here they were.

His mother, a tall but slender woman with no-nonsense gray hair and dark-rimmed glasses, aimed a hesitant smile his way before pulling his stepfather into a pew. He was surprised they'd come, but more surprised at how glad he was to see them. But before he could analyze that development Jessica started down the aisle and he forgot everything but her.

She looked like an angel as she floated toward him through the sacred space, completely at home among the statues of saints and stained-glass windows. Maybe she was—his Irish ancestors had certainly believed in otherworldly beings. But when she put her hand in his it was warm and real. And he was going to hold on for the rest of his life.

He promised as much in their vows, the words almost the same as last time. But that was the only similarity. Next to him, Jessica's smile never faltered, even when her eyes shined with unshed tears. Behind him were their friends and three generations of family. This was how it was supposed to be. He'd have to thank Mrs. Santiago—no, she'd said to call her Elena now—for making it happen.

"I now pronounce you man and wife…again." The elderly priest said with a wink. "You may kiss your bride."

He'd been waiting all day for this, and he took his time with it. Carefully he explored her mouth, taking his fill while hoots of laughter and a few "get a rooms" echoed around them, mixing with the smell of incense and the taste of her lips. Sensory overload, in the best way possible.

Finally, the old priest pointedly cleared his throat, and Jessica pulled back, laughing. He might have tried for another kiss, priest or no priest, but his wife reached for Matthew before he got a chance. It was time to move on to the baptism.

"Would the godparents please come forward?" asked the clergyman as he scanned the small crowd. Cassie and Alex complied, taking their places at the altar as rehearsed.

Maybe it was a sudden prick of conscience, maybe it was divine intervention, or maybe it was just a need to make sure their new start didn't carry over any old baggage. But he heard himself ask, "Would it be possible to have multiple godparents?"

"Hmm?" The pastor pushed his glasses up his nose, his eyes scrunching as he considered the question. "Well, yes. Normally godparents need to complete a class, but since these two already have I suppose there's no harm in having more. A little extra spiritual support can only be a good thing for the boy."

Perfect.

Ryan turned to his parents, and hoped they'd take the offer in the spirit it was meant, as an olive branch to signify forgiveness and healing. "Mom, Greg, would you be willing to be my son's godparents?"

Shock washed over his stepfather's face, but

only for a moment. He stood eagerly, clutching his wife's hand as he nodded. "We'd be honored to."

Beside him Jessica squeezed his hand in support. The wedding had joined them together, and now the baptism was renewing his bond with his parents. Maybe that's how it always was with new babies; maybe seeing someone so innocent and full of possibilities couldn't help but make you want to be the best person you could be. Having a son had made him want to be a better man, and this was a small step in that direction.

Matthew slept through the ceremony, unaware of the importance of the moment, only opening an eye briefly as the holy water was poured over his head.

"He's a calm one," his stepfather noted, nodding at the baby sleeping in Ryan's arms. They were alone in a corner of the church, waiting for Jessica to change into something more comfortable before heading to her mother's house for refreshments.

"He's been pretty laid-back so far," Ryan agreed. "Although we're not sure where he could have gotten that from. Jessica can be a spitfire, and well…you know me."

"I certainly do. And I know things haven't been good between us. I want to thank you for looking beyond that, and inviting us today, and then asking us to be godparents. It meant a lot to your mother."

He shook his head. "No, it meant a lot to *both* of us. I didn't always tell you when I was proud of you, or when you did a good job, and I'm sorry. You've done well for yourself, Ryan. Your dad would be proud."

"And you, are you proud of me?" He was a grown man, he didn't need anyone's approval, but still he asked.

"Of course I am."

"Even though I'm just a cop, and not some fancy lawyer?"

"I'm proud of you because you set your mind to do something and you did it well." He shrugged. "Yes, I thought you should go to law school, but I shouldn't have pushed so hard. You should know, it was because you showed such an aptitude for it, not because of any disrespect for law enforcement. Hell, as an attorney I work with the police on a regular basis and they are some of the finest people I know. Smartest too."

Ryan's head spun as he made sense of his stepfather's words. "Wait, you thought I had an aptitude for it?"

"Absolutely," Greg answered without hesitation. "When you helped me on that one case the summer before you graduated you had some great insights. You seemed to find it interesting too—at least I thought you did."

Ryan shifted the baby to his shoulder. "It *was* interesting," he admitted. "But I just thought..."

The older man put a hand on Ryan's shoulder in solidarity. "I think maybe we both did too much thinking and not enough communicating. And that's on me," he added. "I was the adult, and I should have done better by you."

"I didn't exactly make it easy." Looking back, he wasn't sure how his stepfather had put up with him.

"No, you didn't," he agreed without a hint of animosity. "But that's the past. I'm much more interested in the present. So how about you introduce me to that pretty bride of yours, and let's just forget the rest." He held out a hand. "Deal?"

"Deal."

"Thank you, I was starving." Jessica accepted the large slice of gooey coconut cake Ryan handed her, balancing the plate on the patio railing.

"I thought you might be. Seemed every time I tried to bring you something to eat you were busy feeding Matthew."

She nodded, her mouth full. Swallowing, she reached for the glass of iced tea he held and stole a sip. "I think he's having a growth spurt or something."

"Well he'd better not grow up too fast—I'm

still getting used to this daddy thing. Seems there's quite a learning curve."

"Oh, please, you're a pro already. But speaking of parents, I saw you talking with your stepfather earlier back at the church. How did that go?"

Ryan leaned back against a pillar, his posture more relaxed than she'd seen in some time. "Really well, actually. We both apologized for the arguments we had in the past, and agreed to do better. He even said he's proud of me for being a cop." There was wonder in his voice, and her heart ached for the boy who'd felt so rejected for so long.

"So he's not still angry that you aren't a lawyer?"

He shook his head. "Nope. And he said the reason he'd pushed me toward law school was because he thought I'd like it, that I'd be good at it."

"Of course you'd be good at it." She thought of the shelves full of legal texts and crime novels in the living room. "And you definitely do have an interest in the field."

He shrugged. "I always have. I'd kind of kicked around the idea myself, at one point. But then—"

"But then your stepfather, who you resented, told you to…"

"And so out of spite I shut down the idea. Becoming a cop instead was my way of proving to him who my real father was, who I wanted to be like." He grinned ruefully. "Pretty dumb, huh?"

Scooting closer, she set down her plate and wrapped her arms around him. "Not smart, maybe, but understandable. You were young, and you were hurting." She looked up at him, a thought striking her. "It's not too late, you know. You could still go to law school. Plenty of cops do." Her brain whirred though the possibilities. "I could go back to work, and you could enroll in classes. You'd be home a lot more than you are now, and my mom said she'll help with the baby."

His eyebrows raised in surprise. "Are you serious?"

"If you want to do it, why not?"

"For starters, even if I got a stipend or scholarship, we can't afford to lose my salary."

"We have my inheritance."

"No." He shook his head, the light going out of his eyes. "That money is yours. I'm not going to take it."

"It's ours," she argued. "Consider it an investment in our future."

"I don't know that I could feel right about that, Jess."

"Well, figure out a way. Because if there's anything I've learned from this whole mess, it's that we shouldn't let money interfere with our happiness. If going to law school would make you happy, you should do it. No regrets."

"You really mean it?" He sounded like a kid being given a puppy, as if he couldn't quite believe something so good could be true.

She nodded, happy to think that the inheritance that had come so close to driving Ryan away would be used to make him happy. "I do. Think of it as business deal. In a few years time you'll graduate and pass the bar, and then I'll have free legal advice whenever I want."

"Don't you already get that from Dani?"

"Hmm…good point." She snuggled up against him, loving how perfectly they fit together. "Maybe you'll have to come up with some extra incentive, you know, to beat out the competition."

He leaned down and nuzzled her neck. "I'm pretty sure I can come up with something." His breath tickled her ear, sending tingles of awareness down her spine. "So what do you say—is it a deal? Are we partners?"

Her mind flashed back to when he'd suggested a different deal on this same porch. She'd accepted that one out of desperation. This time, she had nothing but confidence—in him, in herself, and in their love for each other. "Yes, partners. Forever."

* * * * *

Don't miss previous books from Katie Meyer:

The Groom's Little Girls
A Wedding Worth Waiting For
Do You Take This Daddy?
A Valentine for the Veterinarian
The Puppy Proposal

All available now from Harlequin Special Edition!

COMING NEXT MONTH FROM

H HARLEQUIN
SPECIAL EDITION

Available January 26, 2021

#2815 WYOMING CINDERELLA
Dawson Family Ranch • by Melissa Senate

Molly Orton has loved Zeke Dawson since middle school. And now the scrappy single mom is ready to make her move. Except Zeke wants Molly to set him up with her knockout best friend! Molly knows if Zeke spends more time with her and her adorable baby, he'll see what love *really* looks like. All this plain Jane needs is a little Cinderella magic...

#2816 THEIR SECOND-TIME VALENTINE
The Fortunes of Texas: The Hotel Fortune • by Helen Lacey

Kane Fortune has never had any trouble attracting women—he's just never been the type to stick around. Until he meets widowed mom Layla McCarthy and her adorable toddler. But Layla's worried he's not up to the job of *lifetime* valentine. Kane will have his work cut out for him proving he's right for the role.

#2817 THE HOME THEY BUILT
Blackberry Bay • by Shannon Stacey

Host Anna Beckett knows clear well the Weaver house has never been a functioning inn, but taking the project got her to Blackberry Bay...the only place she'll ever find answers about her own family. Will her secrets threaten the budding romance between her and fake handyman Finn Weaver?

#2818 THE COWGIRL'S SURPRISE MATCH
Tillbridge Stables • by Nina Crespo

To keep the secret wedding plans from leaking to the press, Zurie Tillbridge and Mace Calderone must pretend *they* are the ones getting married. Cake tasting and flower arranging seem like harmless fun...until wary workaholic Zurie realizes she's feeling something real for her fake fiancé...

#2819 A SECRET BETWEEN US
Rancho Esperanza • by Judy Duarte

Pregnant waitress Callie Jamison was settling in to her new life in Fairborn, Montana, dividing her time between the ranch and the diner...and Ramon Cruz, the sexy town councilman, who never fails to show up for the breakfast shift. But will he still feel the same when he learns the secret Callie has been keeping?

#2820 HER MOUNTAINSIDE HAVEN
Gallant Lake Stories • by Jo McNally

Jillie Coleman has created a carefully constructed world for herself, complete with therapy dog Sophie, top-of-the-line security systems and a no-neighbors policy at her mountaintop retreat. But when intriguing developer Matt Danzer shows up, planning to develop the abandoned ski resort on the other side of the mountain, Jillie finds her stand-alone resolve starting to crumble...

YOU CAN FIND MORE INFORMATION ON UPCOMING HARLEQUIN TITLES, FREE EXCERPTS AND MORE AT HARLEQUIN.COM.

HSECNM0121

*Jillie's a bestselling horror writer who wants to be left
alone in her isolated mountainside cabin. Matt bought
the abandoned ski resort next door and plans to reopen
it. These uneasy neighbors battle over everything...*

Read on for a sneak peek at
Her Mountainside Haven,
*the next book in the Gallant Lake Stories
by Jo McNally.*

"And your secluded mountainside home with the
fancy electronics is part of that safety net? And your
hellhound?"

Jillie chuckled, looking up to where Sophie was
glaring down at Matt from the deck. "Don't insult my
dog. She's more for companionship than protection.
Although her appearance doesn't hurt." She shuddered
and pulled her jacket tighter.

God, he'd kept her standing out here in the cold and
dark while he grilled her with questions. She'd already
hinted that it was time for him to go. He scrubbed his
hands down his face.

"I'm sorry, Jillie. You must be freezing. Go on up.
Once I know you're inside, I'll take off."

"And you were on your way to dinner. You must
be starving." She hesitated for just a moment. In that
moment, he *really* wanted her to invite him up to join

her for dinner, but that didn't happen. Instead, she flashed him a quick smile before turning to go. "Thanks again, Matt."

Let her walk away. Way too complicated. Just let her walk away.

She was all the way up to the deck when he heard his own voice calling out to her.

"The old ski lift is working well, but I need to give it a few test runs, just to get acquainted with the thing. If you want a ride up to that craggy summit you like so much, I'll be heading up there Sunday afternoon. It'll just be us. No workers. No spectators."

Her head started to move back and forth, then stopped. She looked down at him in silence, then gave a loud sigh. "Maybe. I'll let you know. I've…I've got to go in."

He watched her and Sophie go through the door. She turned and locked it, then gave him a stuttering wave. For someone obsessed with privacy, it was interesting that this entire wall, right up to the peak of the A-frame roof, was glass. He lifted his hand, then headed to his car. He wasn't sure what surprised him more. That he'd asked Jillie to ride to the top of the mountain with him, or that she'd said maybe. As he turned the ignition, he realized he was smiling.

Don't miss
Her Mountainside Haven *by Jo McNally,*
available February 2021 wherever
Harlequin Special Edition books and ebooks are sold.

Harlequin.com

Get 4 FREE REWARDS!

We'll send you 2 FREE Books plus 2 FREE Mystery Gifts.

Harlequin Special Edition books relate to finding comfort and strength in the support of loved ones and enjoying the journey no matter what life throws your way.

FREE Value Over $20
